Bad Boy fireman Singer

Off-Limits Small Town Romance

T.S. Fox

T.S. Fox

Contents

C HAPTER ONE
MANNY

For a man whose job is literally to fight fires, I sure loved running into them.

In my world, danger was a dance partner, and I embraced it with everything in me. The rush of adrenaline, the crackling chaos that surrounded me—it was addictive, intoxicating. Most people shy away from danger, but not me. I welcomed it like an old friend.

The flames roared like thunder, their furious orange and red tongues licking at the sky. The fire's fury mirrored something within me—a wild, untamed spirit. The building was a high-end restaurant that had been apparently reserved for the night by some singer. Most of it had been destroyed by the fire though.

Captain Rodriguez's voice broke through the crackling sound as he jogged over to me. "Manny, Elena Foster is still stuck in there!"

I frowned. Who the hell was that?

"Don't worry, Cap. I'll get her out," I said anyway.

Without wasting another second, I charged into the building. The inferno raged around me, but I felt invincible, alive. Flames flickered, their orange hues casting eerie shadows on the walls.

As I advanced further into the blaze, the intense heat pressed against my skin. My heart pounded and I strained my ears. And then I heard it—a voice, a woman's voice, sharp and frantic. I followed the sound, to what looked like the restrooms. The smoke stung my eyes as her cries grew louder.

Finally, I spotted her—a figure huddled in a corner, the dim light revealing her distress. She was alone, her sobs echoing in the confined space. Flames danced around her. It had to be her. She was the only one left.

"Hey!" I called out over the roar of the fire. "I'm here to get you out."

Her eyes were tightly shut, her face contorted with fear. I rolled my eyes at her reaction—closing her eyes was hardly going to make the situation any better. With swift movements, I closed the distance between us.

"Miss, please open your eyes," I coaxed, my voice softer now. I had to find a way to break through her panic. Gently, I reached out and touched her arm. "I've got you but I need you to stay alert."

Her body felt fragile in my grasp, and I lifted her with ease. As I carried her, she clung to me, her grip desperate and trembling. She murmured something unintelligible, her breath hitching in her throat.

"What was that?" I asked.

She hesitated, her voice barely audible. "I don't want to die."

I paused for a moment, my grip on her tightening, my eyes searching her face in the dim light. I saw the fear etched into her features, even though her eyes were still closed.

"You're not going to die," I said. Then I adjusted my hold on her, cradling her against my chest. Her body was tense, her breath uneven, and I was acutely aware of the weight of responsibility on my shoulders. I couldn't let her down—I wouldn't.

I turned around and moved through the inferno. The heat pressed against me, as I scanned our surroundings for a new path to safety. I knew I couldn't afford to fail; her life depended on it.

Then, a glimmer of hope—a different exit, framed by flames but not entirely consumed by them. I licked my lips and sighed in relief. "Hold on tight," I told her, my voice unwavering. "We're going through there."

Her grip on my jacket tightened as I approached the fiery passage. The flames licked at the edges and I took a deep breath, the acrid scent of smoke filling my nostrils, before stepping into the searing heat.

As we navigated through the wall of fire, I could feel its intensity pressing against my skin, but I pressed on. I was Manny Delgado, and I could conquer anything. "Almost there," I muttered, more to myself than to her.

And then, we walked out from the flames, into a space filled with thick smoke that seemed untouched by the fire. I squinted my eyes and glanced around. "I'm going to have to put you down," I said to the woman, my voice low and steady.

She finally opened her eyes and they met mine, her hesitation evident, but she nodded slowly, her grip on me loosened. I carefully set her on her feet, my gaze locking onto hers. "Stay close," I urged. "We're almost out."

Turning away from her, I focused on the door that stood before us. With a swift, powerful kick, I aimed for the doorknob, my boot connecting with a resounding thud. But the door held fast.

Gritting my teeth, I gave it another fierce kick. It protested, but I could feel it beginning to give way. My third kick was met with a resounding crash.

As the door finally gave, I turned to the woman, extending my hand towards her. "Grab my hand," I urged.

She reached out, her fingers intertwining with mine, and together, we stepped out into the clear night air. The contrast between the smoke-filled room and the cool outside was almost surreal.

We walked out of the building and I sighed in relief. We had come out from the side and as we walked out front, I glanced around. A crowd had gathered in front of the restaurant—firefighters, onlookers, and even a cluster of what seemed to be journalists with cameras at the ready.

"What the hell?" I muttered under my breath, my brow furrowing. This was supposed to be a routine rescue, but it seemed like the whole world had turned its attention to this particular fire.

Right. Captain had said the woman was a celebrity.

She let out a shaky breath beside me, her grip on my hand tightening. I glanced down at her. I had been so focused on getting us both out alive that I didn't have a chance to really take a look at her, but now, her face was illuminated in the glow of the flames, and I couldn't help but be struck by her presence.

My gaze met hers, and I felt something deep within me shift. Her eyes were a vibrant shade of green, like the lush hue of a forest, and they were framed by long, fluttering lashes that seemed to draw me in. My eyes widened. Wow, she was gorgeous. Her lips were set in a determined line even as she trembled slightly. She didn't look like she was my age though.

"Elena Foster!" Someone screamed from the crowd.

I blinked, realizing that I had been staring. Heat crept up my neck, and I cleared my throat, shifting my attention back to our surroundings.

I removed my helmet, the weight of it suddenly feeling much lighter as the flames crackled around us. The woman—Elena, as I now knew her—looked up at me with those enchanting forest-green eyes. "Thank you," she murmured, her voice soft amidst the chaos.

I shrugged off her gratitude with a nonchalant grin. "Don't mention it," I replied, my tone casual as I motioned toward the crowd of firefighters and emergency personnel. "You should go get checked out by a medic."

I took a step back and motioned to head back to the truck. But as I moved away, I felt a tug by my side. I turned back, my brow furrowing as I glanced at Elena, who was holding onto my gear.

My eyes met hers. Was she hurt? What was going on? Why was she holding me back?

"Elena Foster!" Another voice from the crowd pierced the air, calling out her name. She seemed to be well known, not by me but by a lot of people too. I wondered what she did.

She ignored the crowd, her attention fixed on me. Then she took a step closer, and I felt a strange heat creeping up my neck. What was she doing? I blinked at her, my head tilting slightly, my words caught in my throat. "What's the problem?"

The noise from the crowd seemed to fade into the background, replaced by the thudding of my heart in my ears. Her gaze was unrelenting, her eyes captivating, and before I could react, her lips were on mine.

Time seemed to stop as her kiss washed over me, unexpected and electrifying. I froze in place, my mind struggling to catch up with what was happening. The crowd erupted into cheers, their voices merging into a distant cacophony that was barely audible over the rush of blood in my veins.

Her kiss deepened, and I could feel the intensity of it coursing through me. Her tongue slipped into my mouth, and my body reacted before my mind could fully process the sensation. My hands remained suspended in the air, unsure of where to land, while hers found their way to my hair, her grip surprisingly firm.

When she finally released me, I blinked at her, feeling both confused and surprised. I opened my mouth to say something, to demand an explanation, but the words wouldn't come. My thoughts were a jumbled mess, and I was left standing there, my lips tingling from the taste of her kiss.

Wow. She was such a good kisser.

The sudden arrival of medics and guards broke the spell, their urgent voices pushing their way through the fog in my mind.

"Miss Foster, are you okay?" One of them asked as they moved to whisk her away, and I found myself rooted to the spot, my gaze locked onto Elena as she was led away.

What the hell just happened?

CHAPTER TWO

ELENA

Sitting in the backseat of the car, I stared out the window, my thoughts a tumultuous mess. The world outside was passing by in a blur, but I barely registered it. My own music played softly through the speakers and I recognized the voice that flowed from the speakers—the voice that used to be mine. The voice of a younger Elena, naive and hopeful, singing about love and passion. I clenched my jaw, hating the sound of my own voice and the sentiment behind the lyrics.

"Turn it off," I muttered, my voice edged with frustration. The driver complied without a word, and the car fell into an uneasy silence. I leaned back against the seat, my gaze still fixed on the passing scenery, but my mind was miles away from the picturesque Baileys Harbor.

A sigh sounded beside me, and I turned my head to see Cookie, my best friend, watching me with concern in her eyes. I managed a weak smile, though it didn't reach my eyes. "I'm fine," I assured her, though even I could hear the lack of conviction in my voice.

"Of course, Elena," Cookie replied, her tone gentle but knowing. She was always there, always ready to support me, but now I wasn't sure if her support could get me through this.

My life was a mess.

Two days had passed since that night— the night when I broke up with Caleb, the night when I almost died in a fire after he left. It was as if the universe had conspired to send my life spiraling into chaos.

As the car continued to move, I shifted my gaze to the window again, watching the buildings and trees blur together. The world outside seemed so normal, so unaffected by the turmoil inside me. I envied that sense of normalcy, that ability to go about life without being haunted by mistakes and regrets.

"We're almost home," Cookie said softly.

I nodded, not trusting my voice to respond. But I didn't want to go home. The prospect of returning home felt suffocating. I didn't want to face the quiet walls that held memories of a time when things were simpler. No, going home wasn't what I wanted right now. What I wanted was to disappear.

I turned to Cookie to tell her. But as I glanced at her, I saw that she was engrossed in an article on her tablet. My curiosity got the better of me, and I leaned closer to see what she was reading.

My heart skipped a beat as I saw the picture on her screen. It was a shot taken outside the burning restaurant, capturing the exact moment when I had kissed the firefighter. My face flushed with embarrassment, and I covered my burning cheeks with my palms.

"Are people still talking about that?" I asked, my voice filled with mortification.

Cookie looked up from the tablet, her eyes twinkling with amusement. "Oh, they definitely are," she confirmed, a hint of laughter in her tone.

I sank back into my seat, my cheeks still burning as I thought about that impulsive, reckless kiss. It had been a moment of madness. I had been so overwhelmed by everything—the breakup with Caleb, the near-death experience, the chaos surrounding my life—that I had acted without thinking. And now, the whole world had witnessed that moment of weakness.

Kissing the fireman had been a foolish decision, one I couldn't fully comprehend even now. But there was no denying that it had left a mark—a mark that was now plastered across the pages of magazines and the screens of countless devices. I hadn't gone online since that day to see what people were saying, but I had a feeling they weren't saying good things.

"Do you want to talk about it?" Cookie asked gently, her voice filled with concern.

I sighed softly, my gaze still fixed on the passing scene outside the window. "No," I replied quietly. What was there to say? What could I possibly explain about a kiss that had been born out of confusion and heartache? It was a moment I couldn't fully comprehend myself, let alone explain to someone else.

I turned my attention to the night sky, my fingers tracing an absent pattern on my thigh. I kissed a man whose name I didn't even know. It was a fleeting moment of weakness, an anomaly, an aberration that had no place in my life. Now, I was going to make him a distant memory. I had no idea where he was, and I hoped I never had to find out.

I felt my cheeks flush with embarrassment as the car slowed down. We were back at my house—the house I had bought when I first moved to Baileys Harbor. It was a grand structure, standing tall and elegant. I had chosen this town for its quiet and calm, for its sense of solace.

Now it felt like I didn't even want to be in it. Caleb had ruined that for me.

"Home sweet home," Cookie said with a small smile, attempting to lighten the mood.

I managed a faint smile in return, but inside, I still felt a knot of unease. My house stood before me. Its exterior was a blend of classic charm and modern elegance—a two-story structure with a white facade adorned with intricate details. The sprawling gardens were a riot of colors, with vibrant flowers and lush greenery framing the house in a picturesque embrace. A cobblestone path led to the grand entrance, where a set of double doors welcomed me home.

I stepped inside. The entryway was spacious, with polished marble floors and a sweeping staircase that led to the upper floors. The walls were adorned with tasteful artwork and photographs, capturing moments from my life and career.

I yawned. "I need to rest."

"You've been resting for two days at the hospital," Cookie said behind me.

"I have," I admitted, my shoulders slumping slightly, "But I feel like I need more rest."

"Well," She said, "You take all the time you need. But... I should let you know that Caleb's been calling."

"I don't want to see or hear from Caleb," I muttered, my voice edged with a mixture of frustration and exhaustion. Cookie looked at me sympathetically.

"He's lucky he had even left the restaurant before the fire started," She remarked as she looked away, her tone carrying a hint of disdain.

I didn't dwell on the thought, not wanting to waste any more energy on Caleb than I already had. With a weary sigh, I continued up the staircase. When I got to my bedroom, I closed the door behind me and leaned against it for a moment. Then I walked further into the room and collapsed onto the bed, my body sinking into the soft mattress.

My gaze drifted up to the ceiling. The events of the past days left me feeling drained and overwhelmed. I wanted to escape, even if just for a moment, from the weight of it all.

My gaze fell on my tablet, resting on the bedside table. And I reached for it and turned it on. The screen illuminated, casting a soft glow in the dim room. I navigated through the device, feeling a bit of unease as I scrolled through articles and notifications.

I clicked on one of the articles that had caught my attention on the tablet. The screen displayed a familiar image, the picture of me and the fireman outside the restaurant.

As I looked at it, I couldn't help but remember the way his lips had felt against mine. It was strange how effortless it had been, as if our lips moved against each other naturally, as if for that brief moment, nothing else existed. My thumb brushed across my lips involuntarily as I replayed the sensation in my mind.

I continued to stare at the picture. The fireman was strong. He was handsome even, with a ruggedness that contrasted with his role as a rescuer. He looked young too, way younger than me in fact.

I let out a breath I hadn't realized I was holding, my cheeks flushed with a mixture of embarrassment and a strange fluttering feeling. I knew I shouldn't be thinking about the kiss, about the fireman who was nothing more than a stranger. I tossed the tablet aside, its screen dimming as it settled on the bed beside me. Then I let out a squeal of frustration, both at my own thoughts and at the absurdity of the situation.

Running a hand through my hair, I sighed and pushed myself up from the bed. It was clear that I needed to distract myself, to focus on something else.

I needed to sleep.

***

The evening light filtered through the curtains, casting a gentle glow across the room. I let out a soft sigh as I stirred in bed, stretching my limbs as I slowly woke from sleep. With a reluctant sigh, I finally pushed the covers aside and swung my legs over the side of the bed. The cool floor met the soles of my feet and as I stood, a sense of heaviness settled over me.

As I made my way down the stairs, my thoughts were a jumbled mess. I still had dreams about being stuck in a fire...about to die. The memories replayed in my mind, like a broken record and they didn't stop until I found Cookie in the living room.

"You're still here?" I couldn't help but sound surprised as I spoke.

She looked up from her tablet, a small smile on her lips. "Of course, I am," she replied. "I'll leave when I'm sure you're okay."

I let out a sigh, my gaze drifting as I contemplated her words. "I'm fine, Cookie," I assured her, though I wasn't sure if I believed my own words.

She arched an eyebrow, clearly unconvinced. "You just need some time off to figure things out," she said gently, her concern genuine.

I nodded. "Yeah, that's exactly what I need," I admitted, running a hand through my hair.

As I took a seat next to her, she adjusted so she was facing me. "Is this about Caleb?" She asked, her voice soft.

I hesitated for a moment before nodding slowly. "Yeah," I replied. "I broke up with him at the restaurant, but he's still my manager and I'm not sure how to navigate that."

Cookie's gaze held mine, her expression thoughtful. "Do you want to fire him?" she asked, her question direct.

I let out a sigh, my shoulders slumping as I considered the question. "I don't know," I admitted. "He cheated on me, but he wasn't a bad manager. In fact, a lot of my success could be attributed to him."

Her response was immediate, her voice firm. "A lot of your success could be attributed to your talent and your hard work," she countered. "You need to start thinking about yourself, Elena. What's best for you."

I took a deep breath. I was grateful that I wasn't alone but maybe Cookie was right. I hadn't thought about myself in years, not about what I wanted or anything else. I made the type of music my fans loved. I did everything Caleb wanted. I even-

"What do you want to do, Elena?" Cookie's voice was gentle, jolting me out of my reverie.

I hesitated for a moment, considering my options. "Honestly, I feel like I need a vacation," I admitted. I wanted to leave Baileys Harbor, leave where everyone knew me so well. I wanted to be alone.

"A vacation?" she repeated.

I nodded slowly. "Yeah, I think I just need some time away, some space to clear my head."

Without missing a beat, Cookie's gaze shifted to her tablet, her fingers tapping away. "Alright," she said, her voice calm. "I'll make preparations for you to go to Whispering Pines."

I blinked, caught off guard by her swift response. "Wait, what?" I stammered.

She looked up at me, her expression unwavering. "Don't worry about the press or anything else," she assured me. "I'll handle it. But if you want a vacation, you should take a vacation. Do some self-care."

Self-care? I hadn't done much self-care in a while.

I let out a sigh, the tension that had been building within me slowly easing. "Are you sure? I mean, with my name on the trend tables and everything, I-"

"You've been through a lot Elena," Cookie's eyes softened as she said to me, "You deserve a break, Elena."

"Okay," I finally conceded, a small smile tugging at the corners of my lips. "Alright, I'll take a vacation."

A sense of relief washed over me, the prospect of a temporary escape from the chaos bringing a glimmer of hope.

"When can I go?" I asked, eager to leave behind the whirlwind that had become my life.

Her lips curved into a knowing smile. "Tomorrow," she replied.

Tomorrow—just one more day, and then I would be far from the prying eyes of the media and the complications of my personal life. There would be no paparazzi, no Caleb and definitely no mistakes with hot firemen.

CHAPTER THREE
MANNY

I sat in the fire station, quickly cleaning my gear. We had a fire drill in half an hour and Omar didn't like tardiness.

Omar was the best fireman at the station and he was currently acting as Captain since our actual Captain, Rodriguez was on his honeymoon with his wife. It made sense that Omar would take charge after Captain Rodriguez left but the guy had way too many rules to keep up with.

"Hey, rockstar!" A voice cut through the air and I turned around to see Jonathan, one of the firefighters. I couldn't help but roll my eyes. They'd dubbed me "rockstar" after the incident with Elena Foster.

I glanced up as Jonathan approached, a mischievous grin on his face. "How's Elena?" he asked, his tone lighthearted.

I let out a grunt. He was standing with a few other firefighters and I wasn't in the mood for their teasing. I looked away and continued to clean my gear.

Jonathan chuckled and clapped me on the back before sauntering off with the other guys. As they walked away, I overheard one of them mutter, "Man, I wish a woman like Elena would have kissed me."

"Me too man," another one said, "You know what they say about older women."

My jaw tightened at their comments, but I didn't say anything. Instead, I was left alone in the space. The whole thing with Elena Foster had been confusing from the start. One moment, I was just doing my job, saving a woman from a dangerous situation, and the next, she was kissing me—impulsively and passionately.

I shook my head, trying to clear my thoughts. The memory of her lips on mine lingered, and I couldn't deny that she was an amazing kisser. Her kiss had been gentle and sweet, but she was a stranger.

I knew next to nothing about her, other than what I'd learned from a quick internet search. Elena Foster was a popular singer, a celebrity in her own right. She made pop music and I was more into rock music.

No wonder I knew nothing about her.

The fire drill blared in a flash of sound, jolting the fire station into controlled chaos. I moved quickly, the familiar rhythm of the drill a dance I knew by heart. It was exhilarating, the adrenaline coursing through my veins as we simulated our response to a fire. But no matter how thrilling the drill was, nothing quite matched the rush of a real situation—a new fire, danger looming, and lives to save.

As the drill wrapped up, I grabbed my water bottle, taking long gulps. Leaning against the wall, I let out a satisfied sigh. There was a reason I did what I did, why I chose this career. The thrill, the danger—it was all a part of it. Nothing else could come close.

Well, there was one thing that did that recently—the unexpected kiss with Elena Foster. The memory of her lips on mine sent a shiver down my spine, a sensation I hadn't experienced in a while. But as much as the kiss had given me a rush, I had to admit, the drama that came with it wasn't worth it.

I took another sip of water. Every time I stepped out of the firehouse, people recognized me as the guy Elena had kissed. Suddenly, I was associated with her, as if we were close friends or something. The absurdity of it was mind-boggling.

Just the other day, I saw an old, unflattering picture of myself from high school posted on Twitter. The caption read, "This is the guy Elena is with?" I rolled my eyes at the memory. Sure, I'd been in my goth phase back then, and that picture was far from representative of who I was now. I'd grown, changed, and evolved since then, but now people were bringing up old ugly pictures of me because of Elena Foster.

I let out a huff of frustration, scrubbing a hand through my hair. It wasn't like I had any control over what people posted or said, but it irked me nonetheless. The thrill of that kiss with Elena Foster wasn't enough to outweigh the unnecessary drama. And it wasn't my fault. I didn't kiss her. She kissed me.

She was the one who needed to fix it.

After work, I left the fire station. I climbed into my car and tried to figure out how I could possibly get in touch with Elena Foster. It wasn't like celebrities made it easy for regular folks like me to reach out to them. She was a big deal and I could tell as I scrolled through her social media accounts. They didn't even seem like they were managed by her.

Perhaps I could get a hold of her manager or publicist. It was a long shot, but it was worth a try. I decided to do it when I got home. Turning my attention back to the road, I drove to a nearby store to grab some food for dinner. The store's bell chimed as I entered, and I instinctively reached for the hat and sunglasses I'd bought recently to avoid the unwanted attention that had come my way after the incident with Elena.

Inside the store, I moved swiftly, picking up some essentials: a microwaveable meal, a bag of chips, and a bottle of water. It wasn't gourmet, but it would do the job. At the checkout counter, I paid for my items and headed back outside.

As I made my way to my car, the bustling sounds of the store faded into the background. That's when I heard it—a faint clicking sound, like the snap of a camera. I glanced around, searching for the source of the noise. Was it just my imagination, or was someone actually taking pictures of me?

I opened the car door and placed the food items on the passenger seat. Then I glanced around discreetly, trying to pinpoint the source of that clicking sound. There it was—a figure crouched in a small bush not far from where I stood. Holding a camera, the paparazzo was clearly trying to take pictures of me.

I took a deep breath before I shut the car door and began striding toward the bush, my heart pounding with adrenaline. As I closed in, the paparazzo looked up and scrambled out of the foliage, his camera dangling from a strap around his neck.

Without hesitation, I ran after him. The parking lot was a maze of vehicles and obstacles, but I was laser-focused on the man in all black. He was fast, but I was faster. I closed the gap between us quickly.

Just as he reached the edge of the parking lot, I launched myself forward, tackling him to the ground. We tumbled together, his shouts of protest echoing in my ears.

"Hey man! Stop! Get off me!" He yelled, "This is harassment!"

"Taking unauthorized photos of me is its own form of harassment," I retorted.

With a swift move, I wrestled the camera from his grasp and climbed off him, keeping a firm grip on the device.

He was disheveled and angry. "Give it back," He demanded as he stood from the ground.

I shot him a glare. "If you come any closer, I'll smash this thing to bits!"

He rolled his eyes and rubbed off some dust from his clothes. "My name is Felix Woods. I'm a reporter from New York," he said.

I groaned. A reporter was following me now?

"I'm just doing my job, man," He said, "Give me back the camera."

"No," I held it up farther away from him, "Your job is invading people's privacy?"

"It's more about uncovering the truth, you know?" He said in a defensive tone. "Elena Foster's a big deal, and people want to know what's really going on between her and her sugar baby."

I grimaced, giving Felix a look of utter incredulity. "What the hell are you talking about?" I demanded, my voice laced with irritation.

He shrugged. "Look, man, I've got sources, and they've got their own angles. The public's hungry for scandal, and I'm just delivering. I saw that you got a few things in the store. Where you headed next? To meet up with Elena?"

I scowled, "What?"

"My sources say she's at some place called Whispering Pines," He said, "But I haven't verified that. I will though once I find out if you're going to meet her there."

I blinked at him. Well, finding Elena was easier than I thought it would be. If the reporter was right and she was at that place, then I could just go see her myself. I could also find out a whole lot more from this reporter.

"I'll give you the camera back," I said, "But you have to answer a few questions. First, tell me about this sugar baby thing."

"Your name is Manuel Delgado and you're 10 years younger than Elena Foster. Haven't you heard about the speculations that she may be paying you to spend time with her? Although, I'm not sure how that would work considering her relationship with her manager, Caleb. I was hoping you would tell me about that," Felix shoved his hand into his pocket and pulled out his phone. "Name your price and I'll pay it as long as you tell me what the deal is."

Woah what?

I hesitated. His eyes glinted with something. "She's the one who made headlines with that kiss, you know," he said. "Drama sells, my friend. I suggest you take my offer."

"How did you find out where Elena is?" I asked, changing the topic for a moment.

"One of her bodyguards is my friend, Eugene," he said casually. Then he winked. "You can be too," he said.

I couldn't believe the audacity of this guy. Not only had he invaded my privacy and tried to twist my connection with Elena into some scandal, but now he was attempting to bribe me for information. I took a deep breath.

"First of all, I'm not anyone's sugar baby," I said firmly. "And as for Elena, we're not what you're making it out to be. I don't even know the woman."

Felix's smirk faded slightly, and he seemed to be considering his next move. I watched as he retrieved his phone, his fingers tapping on the screen for a moment.

"Look, Delgado," he began, his tone slightly less condescending, "I get that you're trying to protect Elena, but the truth always comes out eventually. If you want to have a say in how this story unfolds, it's in your best interest to cooperate."

I couldn't help but burst into laughter, a mix of incredulity and frustration bubbling up within me. The absurdity of the situation hit me like a ton of bricks. I was a fireman. I lived a relatively normal life and yet, here I was, caught in the crosshairs of a ridiculous media circus.

I took the camera in my hands and slammed it against the ground with force. The metallic thud echoed and Felix's screams filled the air. Anger surged through me. I wasn't just going to sit while some dumb reporter took pictures of me.

I delivered blow after blow to the camera with my boots, reducing it to a jumble of broken pieces.

"Stop! I don't have those saved," Felix's panicked cries filled the air. I didn't care.

"Bastard!" His shout was laced with anger and desperation.

I shot him a cold glare. "Stay the hell away from me," I growled.

Leaving him behind, I walked back to my car, my pulse still racing from the encounter. My hands trembled slightly and as I slipped into the driver's seat, I gripped the steering wheel, taking a few deep breaths to calm myself.

This was a mess I never asked for. I shouldn't have to deal with this nonsense. As I pulled out of the parking lot, I realized that Elena Foster was the one needed to fix this. She was the one who got me into this and luckily for me, now I knew where to find her.

---- -

CHAPTER FOUR
MANNY

I took deep breaths as I trudged through the falling snow. Surrounded by towering pine trees and nestled on a slope, Whistling Pines exuded a rustic charm that blended seamlessly with the winter landscape. The wood beams of the cabin's exterior contrasted beautifully with the white snow-covered ground. I took a moment to appreciate the untouched beauty of the surroundings, the serenity of the forest, and the way the snow seemed to muffle every sound.

It had been a week since I met Felix and, in that time, the snowfall had begun and intensified. I had to park my car a bit away from the cabin due to the accumulating snow. The cold air nipped at my skin, and I zipped up my jacket a little higher. With each step I took, the snow crunched beneath my boots, and my breath created small clouds in the frosty air.

Work at the fire station kept me busy but Omar was nice enough to let me off for the weekend. I wasn't going to question why he allowed it because at least it gave me time to find out where Whispering Pines was and drive out of town.

I wondered what Elena was doing here in this remote place, if she was here. Hiding? While I suffered under the watchful gaze of the public eye? Did she even know that there were speculations about me being her sugar baby?

Felix had proven to be more persistent than I had initially thought. I'd been cautious, constantly checking my surroundings to ensure I wasn't being followed. The last thing I needed was to be caught by a paparazzo while trying to visit Elena, and fueling more speculations and rumors about us.

My phone vibrated in my pocket, startling me out of my thoughts. I pulled it out and saw the name "Bethany" on the screen. Bethany was a girl I had been seeing on and off, a fun distraction when I wasn't working, but I hadn't been in the mood to speak to her since the night Elena and I kissed. I contemplated answering the call, but ultimately let it go to voicemail. I had other matters to attend to.

Navigating through the snow-covered path, I finally reached the cabin. The sight before me was picturesque, the cabin sitting amidst the tranquil winter landscape. It was eerily quiet, devoid of any signs of life, and I couldn't spot any bodyguards. Weren't celebrities supposed to have security at all times? Doubt started to creep in. Did Felix lie to me? Was Elena here?

My footsteps softened as I neared the cabin. Then suddenly, a noise from inside caught my attention, and I instinctively moved to hide behind a nearby tree. Peering through the branches, I watched as the door swung open, revealing Elena herself.

My heart raced a little faster at the sight of her. She held her phone up to the sky and I watched as she stared at the screen with a mixture of hope and frustration, her lips forming a pout that, strangely, I found adorable.

As she stepped outside, the snow crunching beneath her boots, I marveled at her presence. Her skin seemed to glow in the soft light. Her flowing hair trailed behind her, and those forest-green eyes of hers seemed to shine brighter.

After our kiss, I spent hours staring at her pictures online. Elena Foster was undeniably beautiful, even more so in person. She was older than the women I spent time with, but there was an aura of grace and elegance about her that made her look like a true goddess.

Her attention was still fixed on her phone, and I realized she was likely trying to get a signal. I checked my own phone and saw that I was without any service too. Looking up at the sky, I saw that the snowfall had intensified, and the wind was starting to pick up. The weather was taking a turn for the worse. I needed to talk to her and then get out of there.

Elena sighed, her breath forming a white mist in the cold air, and turned to walk back into the cabin. When the door shut, I moved, my mind racing with so many thoughts. Stepping onto the cabin's porch, I hesitated for a moment. She didn't have any bodyguards around, surprisingly.

I stopped in front of the door. Then I rapped my knuckles against the wood, a series of polite knocks. No response. I frowned, giving it, another try, a bit more insistently this time. Still nothing.

I was about to knock again when the door creaked open slowly. A sense of anticipation hung in the air as I expected to see Elena's face appear. Instead, something unexpected happened – a sharp kick struck my face from the side. I yelped in pain as I tumbled to the floor, my hands instinctively clutching my nose. "What the hell was that?" I exclaimed.

Blinking rapidly through the pain, I looked up to see Elena standing there, her expression a mix of shock and horror. She brought her hands to her mouth in disbelief. "Oh my God, I'm so sorry!" she exclaimed.

My confusion only deepened as I struggled to sit up, the throbbing pain in my nose making it difficult to focus. "What the fuck is wrong with you?" I yelled in a frustrating tone.

Elena's gaze met mine. "I thought you were an intruder," she explained, her voice tinged with regret.

"An intruder?" I repeated, incredulous. "Do intruders usually knock before breaking in?"

She shook her head. "I don't know...I just- I'm really sorry."

I held my aching nose, the sting of embarrassment replacing the pain. I couldn't believe I had been taken down by her. "You know," I grumbled, "I didn't think coming here could get any worse."

Elena's expression fell, and she looked genuinely sorrowful. "I truly didn't mean to hurt you. I'm so sorry."

I sighed, feeling a mixture of frustration and reluctance. "Are you really sorry? Or is your presence in my life some cosmic punishment I deserve for something I did?"

She didn't respond immediately. Instead, she lowered her head for a moment. Finally, she looked up at me with an earnest plea in her eyes. "Can you please come inside? I can get you some ice for your nose."

I hesitated for a moment. Then I followed her into the cabin. The warmth enveloped me, contrasting with the chilly outdoors. I glanced around the cabin's interior, absorbing the rustic charm of the place. Elena directed me to the living area and I complied, taking a seat on a worn but comfortable-looking couch.

My nose was throbbing and I rubbed on it slightly, watching her move about the cabin's kitchen area. She walked up to me a few seconds later, holding what appeared to be ice wrapped in a cloth. I accepted it from her and gently pressed it against my sore nose, the cold soothing the ache.

She watched me, her gaze steady and contemplative. When our eyes met, I raised an eyebrow in question. "What?"

She hesitated for a moment before speaking. "I didn't think I'd see you again."

A bitter chuckle escaped me. "Well, at least you recognize me."

She bit her bottom lip. "Of course, I'd recognize you. We're practically on every gossip magazine's front page now," she said.

"And whose fault is that?"

Elena's cheeks flushed, and she looked away, her fingers nervously tracing the edge of the cloth in her hands. Her response was almost sheepish.

"I know, I know, it's just..." She trailed off, her voice softening as she seemed lost in thought. "I'm so sorry about what happened. I mean, I'm only now realizing how hard it must have been for you."

I let out a sigh, my frustration and the cold ice against my nose seemingly competing for my attention. "You have no idea," I muttered, more to myself than to her. "People are acting like we're together now, or something. I can't even go to the store without people recognizing me. It's even more annoying when they act like they're proud of me, as if getting a kiss from you is something to be proud of."

She blinked at me.

My eyes widened. "I didn't- Not that you're not attractive or anything. It's just-" I paused. "I think it's silly that they act like that, like you're some conquest I've acquired."

Elena's eyes softened. "Oh, I guess I can understand that."

I shook my head, a dry laugh escaping me. "For some reason too, everyone seems to think I'm your sugar baby." The words sounded ridiculous even as I said them, my frustration growing.

Her eyes widened in disbelief. "Wait, what? Sugar baby? That's absurd!"

I nodded in agreement. "Tell me about it. A reporter from New York showed up trying to take pictures of me. He also knew you were here which is how I figured it out. You should fire Eugene by the way."

"Eugene? But he's my..."

"Your bodyguard. Yeah, I know. But he's giving information about you to this reporter named Felix from New York."

Elena took a deep breath and her gaze met mine. "I'm sorry..." She paused and looked up at me expectantly.

"Manny," I said.

She smiled, "Right. Manny, I'm sorry. I didn't mean for any of this to happen." She continued, "The night of the fire... I was having dinner with my ex. I'd just found out he had cheated on me, and I had planned to break up with him. After he left, I stayed back. I couldn't sit at the table, so I moved to the restroom to cry in peace."

My eyebrows furrowed as I listened. "And then the fire started," I concluded.

Elena nodded, her gaze focused as if she was reliving those moments. "Exactly. I was trapped in the restroom for a while because the door got jammed."

"Must have been terrifying," I remarked.

"It's no excuse for what happened... I just want you to understand that I was overwhelmed, not really in my right mind," she said, looking away from me.

I found myself silently staring at her. Her vulnerability was palpable. There was a softness about her that I couldn't ignore, and a certain fragility that was both endearing and unsettling. Her voice wrapped around me like a velvet ribbon, and I found myself unintentionally captivated by the way she moved, and the gracefulness in her gestures as she expressed herself.

I nodded slowly. "I get it. It was a chaotic situation." My voice was calmer than I expected.

She sighed and then turned back to him. Her beauty was undeniable—those forest-green eyes seemed to hold a universe of emotions, her lips were the shade of roses in bloom. There was an ethereal quality to her but even as my mind acknowledged her beauty, I couldn't quite shake the feeling that she was too breakable, like a porcelain doll. I almost expected her to shatter with the lightest touch.

"I've been hiding out here, away from the media circus," She continued, "But I'll put out a statement to clarify things, to set the record straight as soon as possible."

I cleared my throat. "Yeah, that would probably help," I replied in a neutral tone.

She looked at me, her gaze searching for something in my expression. "I know this has caused problems for you, and I'm really sorry about that," she said softly.

When I didn't respond immediately, she licked her lips in thought, a gesture so innocent, it triggered a memory—the memory of our kiss outside that restaurant. My heart skipped a beat, and I frowned at my own reaction.

I shifted uncomfortably. "Yeah, it's been...interesting," I finally managed. "You don't have to apologize anymore though. You can just fix it."

Elena's lips curved into a small smile. "I will. Thank you," she said. I nodded again.

The quietude of the cabin was abruptly interrupted by a sudden rattle. The floor beneath me shivered slightly, and I shot up from my seat. "What the hell is happening?" I blurted out, scanning the room.

Elena moved toward the window, her steps graceful but cautious. She peered outside. "It's just the wind," she said, her gaze fixed on the forest beyond. "This cabin is pretty sturdy. It's weathered worse storms than this so don't worry."

I was torn between believing her words and the instinctual unease that prickled at the back of my mind. Still, I couldn't just stay put. I walked up to the door, opened it and stepped outside, only to be met with a sight that made my stomach twist—the sky was darkening rapidly, and ominous clouds were rolling in.

There was going to be a storm.

"What the hell?" I muttered, disbelief lacing my voice. I turned to Elena, who was standing by the door.

"How did you get here?" She asked.

"I drove," I replied, my voice edged with frustration. "But my car is parked at the edge of the forest. You think I can make it back before the storm hits?"

Elena's expression was one of concern as she looked at me. "I do not. And I don't think you'll be able to drive back to Baileys Harbor in this weather either."

I ran a hand through my hair, my agitation palpable. "Unbelievable," I muttered under my breath as I walked back inside and slammed the door shut. I sank back onto the couch, my frustration radiating off me in waves. I cast a sideways glance at Elena, who was standing by the window, her expression pensive. "So, what do we do now?" I grumbled.

She crossed her arms. "You should stay the night," she suggested softly, her eyes meeting mine. "I'm sure the storm will pass, and it'll be better in the morning. You can leave then."

My hesitation was pretty obvious. I didn't want to be stuck in this cabin, not with her. But going out into the storm now would be foolish, and I wasn't exactly familiar with the area.

Despite my reservations, I found myself nodding. "Fine," I muttered. This couldn't be happening. I couldn't believe my luck—or lack thereof. The universe seemed to have an uncanny way of entangling me further in situations I wanted no part of, especially when it came to Elena Foster.

CHAPTER FIVE
ELENA

I woke up early the next morning, the soft morning light filtering through the windows of the cabin. As I moved around the kitchen, preparing breakfast, my mind couldn't help but wander back to Manny. I wondered if he was still asleep, or if the restless night had kept him awake. Last night had been tense, to say the least, and I couldn't shake off the feeling that he was still harboring some resentment towards me.

As I carried a tray with breakfast items, my thoughts churned with uncertainty. Manny had been grumpy and frustrated since he agreed to stay, and I couldn't blame him. The whirlwind of rumors, the intrusive media, and my impulsive actions had turned his world upside down. I knew he didn't like being in the spotlight, especially not in this context.

I walked up to the door of the room where he was sleeping, my hand hesitating for a moment before I knocked. I wondered if I should just leave him be, let him sleep off the frustration, but part of me wanted to bridge the awkwardness that lingered between us.

So, I made him breakfast.

I knocked again and still, there was no response. Pushing the door open gently, I stepped into the room. The sight that greeted me stole my breath away for a moment. Manny lay there, his features softened in slumber. His strong, chiseled jaw was relaxed, and the lines of worry that had marred his face were temporarily smoothed out. Even in sleep, there was an intensity to his presence, a raw masculinity that was impossible to ignore.

I placed the tray on the small bedside table, my fingers lingering on the edge for a moment as I stared at him. The disarray of his dark hair contrasted with the white pillow. He looked handsome, effortlessly so, and I couldn't help but feel a strange mix of emotions—awe, guilt, and a tinge of something I couldn't quite put my finger on.

My gaze wandered over his features, the way his chest rose and fell with each steady breath. I bit my bottom lip, lost in my thoughts. How old was he, really? The question lingered in my mind, and as if on cue, my eyes fell on his wallet resting on the bedside table. The temptation was strong. I was curious. I knew it might be intrusive, but I couldn't resist the urge to know more about him.

I picked up the wallet gingerly, my fingers tracing its edges as I held it in my hand. My heart raced with a mixture of guilt and excitement as I opened it slowly, revealing its contents. My eyes landed on an ID card, and as I read the name, a soft gasp escaped my lips. "Manuel Delgado."

My eyes widened as I took in the information. He was actually 26 years old, a whole decade younger than me. The realization sent a shock through me. I had assumed he was older, given the way he carried himself.

My gaze shifted to the picture on the ID card, capturing his intense dark eyes and the tousled hair that somehow managed to look effortlessly appealing even in a passport photo. A wry smile tugged at my lips. How did he manage to look good in a passport photo? Nobody was ever this flattering in one.

A voice broke through the quiet air. "What are you doing?"

I yelped in surprise, my grip on the wallet slipping from my fingers. It fell to the floor with a thud, and I winced at the noise. I turned to face him, my cheeks flushed with embarrassment. "I... uh, I was just..." I stumbled over my words, my mind racing to come up with an explanation. "I saw your wallet there, and I was..."

Manny's sudden movement as he sat up caught me off guard, and my breath hitched as I watched him pick up the wallet. His frown deepened as he looked at me, and I felt a rush of embarrassment at having been caught snooping.

I stammered out an apology, my cheeks flushing a deeper shade of red. "I'm sorry, I was just... curious."

His voice was calm but tinged with a hint of exasperation. "You could have just asked, you know."

My gaze dropped to the floor as I continued to fumble over my words, repeating my apologies like a broken record. Manny's sigh cut through my rambling, and his words were more gentle this time. "Stop with the apologizing."

I bit my lip, chastising myself. I always had such a bad grip on my nerves. And, as if on cue, I found myself saying "sorry" again.

Manny rose a brow and I winced at my own reflexive response. My cheeks felt like they were on fire as I looked away.

"I made breakfast for you," I said, gesturing towards the tray. My eyes shifted to his face, waiting for his reaction.

His gaze followed my gesture, and he eyed the tray for a moment before finally responding. "Thank you."

I nodded, my lips curving into a small smile. "I hope you enjoy it."

Before Manny could say anything else, I turned and walked quickly out of the room. My heart was racing in my chest. I was flustered and I was acting like a complete mess.

Stepping outside, the frigid air instantly kissed my cheeks, and I welcomed the icy touch as it helped cool the warmth that had crept up from my embarrassment. I took a deep breath, hoping that the brisk air would clear my head and steady my nerves.

However, as I looked around, my eyes widened. The storm was still raging just as fiercely as before, the wind howling through the trees and the snowflakes swirling in the air. If anything, it seemed to have intensified, making the idea of leaving the cabin even more daunting. My heart sank.

Manny was already upset with me for the drama and chaos that had surrounded our kiss. And now, he was trapped here with me, unable to leave due to the storm. I let out a sigh, my breath visible in the cold air.

If I thought he was angry before, it was going to be so much worse now.

***

I glanced at Manny, bracing myself for another round of frustration or anger. He looked outside the window, his hands by his side. And he sighed. He ran his hand through his hair.

"I guess I'm stuck here huh," he said with a designated tone.

I met his gaze as he looked at me.

"I'm sorry," he said. "I assume you wanted to be alone here. I didn't notice any bodyguards so I'm sorry I'm intruding on your little vacay."

I felt a smile tugging at the corners of my mouth. "It's really okay," I reassured him. "I mean, I do enjoy my alone time, and this isn't exactly how I planned to spend it. But I don't mind."

Manny looked unsure but he nodded. He shoved his hand into his pocket and pulled out his phone. "There's no service," he said when he turned on the screen. "But I need to send a message to some of the guys at the fire station."

My own phone lay on the couch in the living space, devoid of any signal too. I looked up and met Manny's gaze again. "We can leave messages and hope they eventually get through once we have service."

The corner of his lips lifted in a small smile.

"I need to text Cookie anyway," I said. If Manny was right about the reporter he met then I wanted Eugene gone immediately. It made me somewhat sad. He was one of my favorite bodyguards, but I was tired of people lying to me.

A puzzled expression crossed Manny's face. "Cookie?" he asked.

I chuckled. "That's just her nickname. She's my best friend and sort of my personal assistant," I explained with a light laugh.

He nodded and then turned around, still staring at his phone.

"You can have the spare room," I suggested. "I've got some spare clothes you can wear too." I added.

Manny turned to me and raised an eyebrow, a hint of curiosity in his eyes. "Should I even ask who these clothes belong to?"

I wondered if I should elaborate. The clothes belonged to Caleb. He and I used to visit the cabin together all the time and he left behind some of his things the last time. Memories of those times flooded back, but I pushed them aside. I decided not to tell Manny about that and simply shook my head. "Don't worry about where they came from." I replied with a soft chuckle, avoiding the details.

I had been half-tempted to burn them all when I arrived at the cabin, but now they could serve a purpose for Manny.

"What about food?" He asked.

"I've got enough supplies to last me quite a while, so we're good on that front."

He scratched his head, his expression somewhat uncertain. "Thanks for letting me stay," he said, his tone a tad awkward.

I shrugged. "It's nothing. It's not like I could just let you go out there."

He nodded. "I'm going to try sending the message now," he said and then headed off to do just that.

I watched him go, a deep breath escaping my lips as I leaned against the doorframe. The reality of the situation was sinking in: I was now going to be stuck alone in a cabin with the man I had impulsively kissed after the fire. It felt like a lifetime ago, yet here we were, brought together by circumstances beyond our control.

The house seemed eerily quiet, the sound of the wind outside accentuating the stillness within. I took another deep breath, my mind racing with thoughts of how long this storm might last. How long could we endure being cooped up together, our awkward interactions hanging in the air like an unspoken tension?

CHAPTER SIX

MANNY

Sitting at the kitchen counter, I dug into the stack of pancakes Elena had prepared. Each bite was a delightful mix of flavors, and I couldn't help but be impressed by her skills. After a few days of being stuck together due to the storm, I had to admit that she made some of the best food I had tasted in a while.

I took another bite of the pancakes, savoring the flavors as they danced on my taste buds.

"These are really nice," I said in a soft tone. "I've noticed that you make really good food."

Glancing up at Elena, I found her looking at me with a faint blush tinting her cheeks. "Thank you," she replied, her voice equally soft. "Cooking is something I enjoy doing in my free time."

I nodded. Then I watched her cut her pancakes with delicate precision and take each bite with an almost regal grace. Unlike me, who rushed through my food, she took her time with it, almost like a prim and proper princess.

"Hey, I've been meaning to ask," I said, breaking the silence. "How did you manage to kick me in the nose when I arrived? That must have taken some kind of skill."

Elena's eyes widened at my question, and she let out a surprised laugh. "Oh, that. Well, I take karate classes and self-defense classes."

I raised an eyebrow, genuinely surprised. "You take self-defense classes? Why?"

Her expression shifted slightly, a brief flicker of pain crossing her eyes before she composed herself. "I had an altercation with a fan once. It wasn't a pleasant experience, and my security team suggested that I learn some self-defense techniques just in case."

I couldn't help but feel a pang of sympathy for her. To think that she had to learn self-defense due to a troubling encounter with a fan was disheartening. Even celebrities didn't have it so easy. "I'm sorry you had to go through that," I said.

After we had finished our meal, Elena stood and took her plate to the kitchen. I was done too so I stood, carrying my plate and following her. "I'll do the dishes," I said.

She glanced at me hesitantly as we both tossed our plates in the sink. "No, it's fine. I'll handle it."

"You let me stay here and prepared food for me," I said as I grabbed the dishwashing soap. "It's the least I can do."

Elena watched as I squirted some over the dirty dishes and ran the tap. As I scrubbed the dishes, she said, "You really don't have to do this, you know."

I glanced over at her, a soapy plate in my hand. "It's fine, seriously."

Reluctantly, she agreed, her "okay" carrying a hint of uncertainty.

I turned to watch her leave the kitchen, watching her retreating figure for a moment before turning my attention to the dishes. The warm water and soap were a stark contrast to the cold forest outside.

I scrubbed the plates and utensils, my thoughts drifting to the storm that had trapped us here. Looking out the window, I watched the weather fluctuate.

The storm seemed capricious, with moments of intensity followed by periods of relative calm. The snow swirled in the wind, creating a mesmerizing dance of white flakes against the backdrop of the dark trees. The forest was shrouded in an eerie, muted light, and the atmosphere looked...heavy.

I took a deep breath. It still wasn't safe to leave, not when Baileys Harbor wasn't so close. I had checked my phone last night and my message to Omar had been delivered but if he responded, I hadn't seen it, because there was no service. I let out a sigh. I missed home and the fire station. This situation, playing house with Elena Foster, was awkward at best.

I could tell she was trying to make me feel comfortable, but we struggled to find common ground for conversation. Every time I caught her staring at me, I found myself wondering what she was thinking. She was famous and probably not used to being around people like me. She didn't act proud though but maybe she thought that way, you know.

I had just finished the last dish and was drying my hands when a loud crash echoed from Elena's room. My heart raced as I rushed to the door, my knuckles quickly finding it, and I called out, "Elena, are you okay?"

Her voice came through the door, soft and hesitant. "Uh, yeah, I'm fine."

She didn't sound entirely convincing so I pushed the door open slightly and peered inside. "I'm coming in."

I stepped into the room and was met with the sight of Elena standing on a tall stool, her hands on her hips, and an expression of frustration mixed with determination on her face. She pressed her lips together and stared at me.

I tilted my head, bewildered, and asked, "What are you doing?"

She sighed, her voice carrying a hint of exasperation. "Last night, my light bulb went off, and I'm trying to change it."

I blinked. "On a stool like that?" I asked. "And do you even know how to do that?"

She nodded confidently, running her fingers through her hair. "Yeah, my dad taught me."

I raised an eyebrow, both impressed and concerned. "Okay, so what happened?"

Elena pointed to the shattered remains of the old bulb and its decorative cover on the floor. "Well, they slipped from my hands and fell."

I sighed internally. "Are you injured?"

"I'm good," She said, "It's nothing. Can you pass me the new bulb though? It's right there on the bed."

"I am not doing that," I said slowly, trying to keep my patience. "Please come down. I'll help you with this."

I walked towards the stool and Elena shook her head. "Oh no, Manny. It's okay," She said, "Please be careful so you don't step on glass."

"I'm wearing shoes," I said, "Get down."

She shook her head and crossed her arms.

I grimaced. Was this her attempt at being stubborn?

"Come down from the stool right now, Elena," I said in a stern tone.

She parted her lips to argue but bit her bottom lip instead. Then she reluctantly started to descend from the stool, but just as she did, it tipped over, and Elena came crashing down.

I rushed forward, instinctively trying to catch her, but I wasn't quick enough. We both ended up on the floor. Elena landed in my arms with a surprised squeal, her hands instinctively grabbing onto my arms for support. For a moment, we were locked in a close embrace, and I couldn't help but look into her eyes. We blinked at each other, our faces inches apart.

I felt a strange sensation in the pit of my stomach. My heart raced as I found myself getting lost in her gaze, unable to look away. I noticed the subtle rise and fall of her chest, her shallow breaths, and the soft scent that surrounded her. She smelled so good, and I couldn't help but be drawn in. Her lips were so close, and I felt myself unconsciously licking my own in response.

She noticed because her eyes flickered to my lips and mine moved to hers. I couldn't help but remember our kiss, how sweet she had been, like the wine she had probably been drinking that night and just as intoxicating. The memory flashed in my mind, and I found myself wondering what it would be like to taste her again, to feel her lips against mine.

I snapped out of my thoughts, clenching my jaw and frowning at Elena. What the hell was I doing? I needed to get a grip on myself.

With an almost irritated tone, I asked, "Are you always this clumsy?"

Elena blinked as if she had just been pulled out of a trance. She cleared her throat, her cheeks turning a shade of pink. "Um, sorry about that. I guess I tripped."

I let out a breath I didn't realize I had been holding. Then we both moved off each other and I gently set her down on her feet, keeping a safe distance between us.

"I'll take care of changing the light bulb," I said, my voice a little gruff. "You should just sit on the bed."

This time, Elena didn't argue. She just nodded and moved to the bed, sitting down with a soft sigh. I focused on the task at hand, retrieving the new bulb and carefully changing it. As the room was once again bathed in soft light, I turned to find Elena watching me. I met her gaze and this time, I felt a strange combination of annoyance and fondness.

"I'll clean up the broken glass on the floor so you just sit there," I said. I noticed a grimace on her face as I spoke and my frown deepened. I studied her slowly. Something was off. She was covering her palm with her other hand, and before I could stop myself, I walked over to her and gently took her hand in mine.

Her skin was soft against mine, and I could feel the tension in her palm. When I looked closely, I saw a cut on her palm. Frustration bubbled up inside me at the sight of her injured hand.

"Would you believe me if I said it's nothing?" Elena's voice broke through my thoughts, and I paused for a moment before shaking my head.

"No," I replied honestly, my tone softer now. "It doesn't look like nothing."

She let out a small sigh.

"What happened?" I asked, my gaze locked on her hand.

Elena hesitated, her eyes avoiding mine for a moment before she met my gaze again. "I got cut by the edge of the decorative light cover. That's why I dropped it."

I resisted the urge to roll my eyes. Of course, she had hurt herself while trying to change a light bulb. "Is it deep?" I asked, gently prying her fingers away from her palm to get a better look.

She shook her head. "No, it's not that deep. There's a first aid box in the drawer in the corner of the room."

I nodded and quickly retrieved the first aid box, bringing it back to her. Kneeling in front of her, I opened the box and began to clean her injury slowly. I could feel her eyes on me as I worked, and it was strange how comfortable I felt in that moment, tending to her like this.

As I cleaned the cut, I couldn't help but ask, "Do you have trouble asking for help?"

Elena's sigh was soft, and she didn't respond immediately. I didn't expect her to. It sounded accusatory coming from me. I continued to clean her wound, my movements careful and deliberate.

"Yes," she finally admitted, her voice tinged with a hint of vulnerability. "Sometimes, it's hard to ask for help from people."

"I get that," I said, as I continued to clean her cut. "I used to find it hard to ask for help too. But I've had to learn over the past year that it's not so bad to reach out."

Elena looked up at me, her eyes meeting mine, and I could see a glimmer of something in them. She nodded, her expression thoughtful. "Yeah, I think I'll have to learn that too. Now that I have the time."

I finished cleaning her cut, placing the used materials back in the first aid box. "You've got the time to figure things out," I said, looking up at her. "You don't have to rush into anything."

Her gaze met mine, and for a moment, I felt a connection between us that was hard to explain. "Yeah, you're right," she said.

I wrapped a bandage around her palm, securing it gently. "There, all done," I said, my voice soft.

A small smile tugged at her lip. "Thank you, Manny."

I met her smile with one of my own. "Anytime. You can use me as a practice dummy if you want," I teased, trying to lighten the mood. "I'm here if you need help."

Elena chuckled, and the sound was like music to my ears. "I'll keep that in mind."

It was strange how just being here, helping her, making her smile, sent warmth through me. And as I looked into her eyes, I couldn't deny the fact that being around her made me feel good, in a way I hadn't felt in a pretty long time.

CHAPTER SEVEN
MANNY

I was really starting to lose it. The storm outside was bad, and my phone was as useful as a brick. No games, no movies, just the howling wind for entertainment. I glanced at my phone again, futilely hoping for a message, but no luck. My message to Omar had been read, but there was no response, which only added to my growing annoyance. Was the asshole really ignoring me?

With a heavy sigh, I tossed it on the table in frustration. I needed something to do, anything to keep my mind from wandering into strange places. Like a certain dark-haired woman with forest green eyes. Being stuck in a cabin with Elena Foster was one thing, but not being able to do anything but focus on her? It was too much.

The sound of a door opening brought my attention back to the present. I glanced over and saw Elena walking into the room, a bright smile gracing her features. I did my best to suppress the urge to groan inwardly. She looked effortlessly gorgeous in a long purple sweater and thick sweatpants. How did she manage to look this good even in casual clothes?

Elena raked her fingers through her wet hair, causing it to fluff up slightly. It looked like it was a bit wet and I knew she had just gotten out of the shower.

"Are you bored?" She asked with a wry smile.

"Am I that obvious?" I replied.

Her chuckle was a sweet melody. "I could hear your sighs all the way from my room," she said.

I didn't know how I felt about the fact that we had gotten closer over the past few days. On one hand, she seemed more comfortable around me, and I, in turn, felt a growing ease in her presence. But on the other hand, her proximity was starting to affect me more than I was willing to admit.

She settled herself on the couch beside me, and I had to fight to keep my gaze from lingering too long on her. Her scent enveloped me, and I couldn't resist taking a deep breath, filling my senses with her.

"Wanna play a game?" Elena asked.

Boredom had left me craving something, anything, to occupy my time so I replied, "Sure, what game?"

She dashed back into the inner part of the cabin, and came back out a short while later, her arms filled with stacked board games.

I blinked in surprise at the collection. "Woah, why do you have so many board games?" I asked as I moved to help her carry some of the games.

"Caleb and I used to play them when we came to the cabin."

Who the hell was Caleb?

I glanced at her and her eyes widened without looking at me. Her smile wavered for a moment, and it was as if she had been caught saying something she shouldn't have.

That reaction sent a strange feeling coursing through me, one I couldn't quite put my finger on. Nor could I understand why I felt it.

I looked away and placed the boxes in my hand on the coffee table in the middle of the living room. "Who's Caleb?" I asked, trying to sound casual.

Elena hesitated for a moment, and her brief pause didn't go unnoticed. She finally answered, "He's my ex."

I clenched my jaw reflexively. So, Caleb was the ex she had broken up with at the restaurant the night I saved her and if I were to guess correctly, he was probably the owner of the clothes I had been wearing. I glanced down at the green hoodie that fit around my body like a tight glove. The guy had taste. And for some reason, that pissed me off.

I frowned. Why was I so bothered?

Elena seemed oblivious to my reaction as she dropped her stack of games onto the coffee table before us. "What would you like to play?" She asked, changing the topic.

I moved to sit in front of the table, crossing my legs as I went through our options. "I'm not patient enough for Monopoly," I said, "And I have no idea how to play chess."

There were a bunch of other games that I didn't recognize as well.

She smiled as she picked up the scrabble box. "How about scrabble?" She asked and her smile was enough to make me smile in return. "Scrabble it is," I said.

Elena moved to spread out the scrabble set on the table. Then she pushed the other board games underneath, giving her space to sit across from me. She pulled her hair into a ponytail, her gaze on the board and I imagined running my fingers through it.

I cleared my throat. What the hell was that?

She looked up at me and flashed a grin. "Manny, how about we add a little twist to our game?"

I raised an eyebrow. "What kind of twist?"

She glanced around the room, as if there was any one else with us, and then leaned in closer, lowering her voice. "A drinking game," she whispered with a sly grin.

My eyes widened. "You drink?"

She leaned away and crossed her arms. "Of course, I drink. How old do you think I am?"

I chuckled. "That's not what I mean."

Elena just seemed refined, or maybe that was the image I had of her in my head. If anyone ever asked me to describe her in four words, they would be refined, delicate, soft and beautiful. Very beautiful. She seemed like the type of person who liked fruit wine and cheese not bitter alcohol.

"Do you have alcohol in the house?" I asked.

She nodded, her eyes lighting up with excitement. Then disappeared into the kitchen for a moment and returned with a big bottle of tequila and two shot glasses. "This was a gift from a friend. I've been saving it for a special occasion."

"And our game of Scrabble qualifies?"

She giggled and I had never wanted to record a sound so I could hear it over and over again until that moment. "I guess," she said, shrugging.

I laughed. "Alright, I'm in," I said. "How do we play this drinking Scrabble game?"

"So uhm," she began, "here's how it goes. If you manage to use all your tiles in one turn, that's a 'bingo,' and the other person has to take a shot. For every word worth over 20 points, your opponent takes a sip of their drink. If someone challenges a word and it's in the dictionary, the challenger takes a sip. If it's not, the person who played the word takes a sip. Got it?"

I nodded, grasping the concept. We poured shots for each of us, placing them within easy reach. As we started the game, the tiles began to fill the board.

Time passed, and with each move, the alcohol began to take its toll. We challenged words, laughed at the ridiculous combinations we came up with, and took sips of our drinks. Elena was surprisingly good at Scrabble, forming high-scoring words with ease. She had me sipping from my glass more often than I had anticipated.

As the game progressed, she maintained her lead. Eventually, she placed her tiles on a triple-word score and grinned triumphantly. "Bingo!" she exclaimed, standing to do a little victory dance.

I chuckled, surrendering with a mock salute. "You win fair and square."

She pumped her fists in the air and giggled, clearly a bit tipsy from the game. The alcohol had its effect on me as well, and as I watched Elena revel in her victory, everything seemed to move in slow motion. Her ponytail swayed with her dance, and her radiant smile drew me in. When she downed another shot of tequila, I couldn't help but imagine what it would be like to kiss her again, to taste the tequila off her lips.

I sighed. Then closed my eyes and shook my head. The alcohol was clearly getting the best of me.

As I reopened my eyes, I saw Elena stumbling, "woah!" She exclaimed.

I moved quickly to catch her as she came tumbling down. And for a brief moment, with her in my arms, we hooked eyes. I smiled. "You're so clumsy," I said softly.

Her entire face was flushed and she giggled. "Sorry Manny," She muttered.

"Don't apologize," I said, my voice barely a whisper. Our proximity felt electrifying, and Elena seemed just as captivated as I was, her gaze fixed on me.

We were lying there on the ground, her in my arms, and her scent surrounded me. It was one of those moments when time seemed to stretch, and I couldn't help but think about kissing her, maybe even doing more. Elena's lips slightly parted, and her eyes softened as her gaze moved from my eyes to my lips. It was as if everything else faded away, and I couldn't tell if it was just the alcohol playing tricks on my mind or if there was something deeper here, something real.

Then she said, "Manny?" a soft, almost whispered sound that broke the spell.

I couldn't do this, not like this. We were too different, in every conceivable way. I cleared my throat and moved away from her, perhaps too abruptly.

"Be careful," I mumbled, more to myself than to her.

Elena stared at me, her expression one of disappointment, or at least that's how I interpreted it. But it couldn't be right, could it? Then she rose gracefully, her movements not as steady as they usually were. The alcohol had taken its toll, evident in the way she swayed slightly on her feet. Her eyes, a tad unfocused, met mine briefly before she turned away.

"Thank you," she said, her voice soft, and brushed her hair from her face. "I'm really tired so I'm going to go to bed first," She added.

I didn't respond. I was still reeling from what just happened. Was I attracted to her? I watched her hurriedly leave the room, moving with a sort of urgency I hadn't seen before. And once she was out of the room, I sighed as my gaze moved to the bottle of tequila.

Drunk Scrabble was a bad idea.

C HAPTER EIGHT
ELENA

I sat on the edge of the bed, gazing out the window at the breath-taking sight of the snow-covered forest. The world outside was a serene wonderland, blanketed in pristine white. Each tree branch bore the weight of the snow, and the entire landscape seemed to shimmer under the soft morning light. It was the kind of peaceful beauty that made me wish I could stare at it for hours. It was so different from the chaos my life had become.

Sighing, I leaned forward and grabbed a pillow, burying my face in it and releasing a muffled squeal of frustration. Why couldn't everything just be as calm and beautiful as that snow-covered forest? My thoughts drifted back to the laughter of last night, to the Manny's laughter during our game of Scrabble. I remembered how infectious it was, the way his eyes lit up, and I couldn't help but think how handsome, how utterly captivating he was.

But it was a weird thought, right? I shook my head then, blaming it on the alcohol. I continued to brush off any peculiar thought about Manny as the night went on. Each time my mind wandered into that territory, I playfully blamed it on the alcohol. It was easier that way, safer. Until I almost lost my footing and he caught me.

As his strong arms held me, our eyes locked, and for that brief moment, it became painfully clear that it wasn't just the alcohol playing tricks on my heart.

I sat there, my heart pounding erratically in my chest, almost drowning out the sound of my own thoughts. Manny's hand rested casually on my thigh, and though it was just a simple touch through the fabric of my sweatpants, it felt like an electric jolt racing through my entire body. A tingling sensation spread from where his hand made contact, making me acutely aware of his proximity. I found myself wishing he would kiss me and this time he could make me feel that sensation everywhere else with just his fingers.

My eyes widened at the sheer audacity of my own thoughts. What was I doing? Manny was a guest in my cabin, a firefighter who had saved me from the fire that fateful night. Our kiss wasn't even supposed to happen, and it was my fault it had. The thought that he could possibly reciprocate what I felt was absurd.

When I woke up, I was glad I didn't have a hangover. I took my time in the shower, delaying the inevitable moment when I would have to face him again. I didn't want to leave my room and confront the unspoken tension that hung in the air between us. I was scared that he would read my thoughts on my face, that he would see the wild desires I was struggling to suppress.

When Manny moved away from me so swiftly, I hate to say it but I felt so disappointed. Of course, he didn't feel the same way. He was ten years younger than I was, a man who had his whole life ahead of him. What could he want with someone like me?

Caleb didn't want me either.

I let out a heavy sigh, wishing I could talk to Cookie. I had sent her a message, letting her know I was safe and that I would wait out the storm. But I hadn't gotten a response from her due to the service. I knew she would be worried and I could only pray she wasn't crazy enough to make her way to the cabin in the storm.

The silence in the cabin was broken by the creaking of a door, and I jumped out of bed, my heart racing. I tiptoed across the room, my bare feet padding softly on the wooden floor, and pressed my ear against the door. Manny's room was just across the small hallway.

The door to his room swung shut with a soft click, and I held my breath, my ear pressed against the wooden surface. Silence settled in the cabin, broken only by the pounding of my own heart. I didn't know why but it felt like I could sense him. There was an inexplicable awareness that he was out there, right in front of my door. My pulse quickened.

Moments later, the faint shuffle of footsteps reached my ears as they moved down the hallway. Manny was heading toward the kitchen. A sigh of relief escaped my lips as I pulled away from the door. Then I scolded myself internally for behaving so irrationally. There was no reason to be scared of Manny, and hiding in my room like a child was absurd.

I couldn't ignore him forever, especially not when we basically lived together in the cabin. The emotions swirling within me were undoubtedly a result of the close quarters and the peculiar bond we had formed over the past few days. My heart and mind were simply tangled up, confused.

Taking a deep breath, I gathered my resolve and made my way out of the room. My steps were tentative as I walked down the hallway, leading me toward the kitchen. And there, as I turned the corner, I saw him. Manny leaned over the counter, his focus locked on the bottle of tequila from last night.

My heart skipped a beat, and I bit my bottom lip nervously. It seemed my heart and mind were persistent.

I forced a smile as I approached Manny, who was giving the tequila bottle an intense glare. "What are you doing?" I asked, my voice light with amusement.

He looked up at me, his expression a mix of discomfort and mild irritation. "Just letting it know that I'm not its biggest fan right now."

I couldn't help but chuckle. "Are you hungover?" I asked.

Manny nodded, his gaze now flickering over my appearance. A warmth rushed to my cheeks, and I averted my eyes for a moment. I was dressed in a cozy sweater and leggings.

"You look... nice," he commented, his words surprising me.

I raised an eyebrow playfully, a flutter of hope stirring within me. "Nice?" I echoed.

He nodded slowly. "Yeah, you don't look like you've got a hangover."

I smiled. Then I brushed off the compliment with a chuckle. "Well, that's because I don't get hungover, no matter how much I drink."

"Never?" Manny asked in amazement.

I nodded confidently, grabbing the tequila bottle from the counter and placing it in a nearby cabinet. I gestured to the barstools. "Take a seat," I insisted, walking to the fridge. Taking two bottles of water, I set them on the counter in front of him. "You need to hydrate."

"Thank you," Manny said as he grabbed the bottles eagerly, cracking one open and taking a long sip.

"You sure you don't want some painkillers?" I offered, raising an eyebrow.

He shook his head, his dark eyes meeting mine. "Nah, I'll be fine. Just need to rest for a bit."

I couldn't resist sighing. "Well, I'm sorry I can't relate," I said with mock sympathy, a grin tugging at my lips.

Manny's eyes widened momentarily before he chuckled. "Gasconading, aren't we?" he retorted.

I laughed, genuinely amused. It was one of the words I had played during our game last night. "You remembered that word? Impressive!"

He nodded, a playful glint in his eyes. "You taught me, so I'm going to use it," he declared, laughing softly.

I joined in his laughter, my heart feeling lighter. "If you want, Manny, I can teach you more big words," I offered teasingly.

He rolled his eyes playfully again, and I couldn't help but smile. Being around Manny felt surprisingly comfortable.

***

I stared at the blank notepad before me, the lines and empty space mocking my creative drought. It had been too long since I'd written a song, and the breakup with Caleb hadn't exactly been an inspiring muse—it had just been painful.

Suddenly, Manny collapsed onto the couch beside me, his presence a surprise that almost made me jump. He smelled of soap, and a hint of stubble graced his chin, something I oddly found myself wanting to touch. His playful smile greeted me, and he asked, "What are you doing?"

I shrugged. "Just working on a song."

He leaned in a little closer, curiosity dancing in his eyes. "Can I see?"

I hesitated for a moment before shaking my head. "I don't like showing incomplete work."

Manny tilted his head, his expression thoughtful. "Alright, later, then." Changing the subject, he admitted, "Honestly, I had no idea who you were when I met you."

"Really?" I couldn't hide my surprise. I was so used to people recognizing me at first sight.

Manny nodded. "Yeah, I listen to more rock than pop, but I gave a few of your songs a listen after... you know."

The kiss.

The kiss that started this whole thing.

I found myself staring at Manny thoughtfully, lost in a whirlwind of thoughts and emotions. It was strange, thinking back to that night when I was hurt and vulnerable, and I'd kissed him, a random man at the time, to ease my pain. That random man was now sitting right in front of me, and my heart was beating wildly, betraying me with its erratic rhythm.

In the beginning, he had been so grumpy and distant, but ever since the day he helped me change that stubborn light bulb, he'd been nothing but sweet. I'd glimpsed a playful side of him that I shouldn't have seen, a side meant for someone else, someone who fit him.

Manny's eyes softened as he blinked at me. "What are you thinking about, Elena?"

The way my name rolled off his tongue made me clench my thighs together.

You. I'm thinking about you and all the things I want you to do with me.

He leaned in closer, and with gentle fingers, he pushed a loose strand of hair behind my ear. My words caught in my throat, and I couldn't bring myself to respond. The air between us crackled with tension.

Suddenly, I stood up abruptly, my heart racing, and muttered, "I'm going to finish that song in my room."

Manny nodded, and as I hurriedly walked away. This wasn't going to work. I couldn't keep ignoring how I felt anymore.

Inside the safety of my room, I shut the door and leaned against it, taking slow, deep breaths to calm my racing heart. My gaze fell on the notebook in my hands. As if drawn by an invisible force, I began to scribble, words flowing from my pen effortlessly. The lyrics formed on the page, a forbidden melody of desires and longing, a yearning for something that was never meant for me but that I wanted all the same, no matter how much I knew it would hurt.

My fingers danced along the paper, and I hummed a soft, haunting tune to accompany the lyrics. A melody that echoed the sensuality that had been building between Manny and me, a melody that whispered of secret stares and hidden desires. With each stroke of the pen, each note on the page, I poured my emotions onto the paper, a torrent of feelings I could no longer ignore.

Because in the safety of my room, I could admit that I wanted him.

I moved to the corner of the room, where my grand piano stood, with elegant curves and polished wood. I took a seat behind it, placing the notepad next to me. My fingers found their place on the ivory keys, and I began to play.

There was a magnetic pull he had on me. And as the music filled the room, I couldn't help but imagine he felt it too. I imagined that there was an undeniable chemistry between us, that he looked at me and wanted me as much as I wanted him.

I lost myself in the music, fingers dancing gracefully across the piano keys as if they had a mind of their own. The melody flowed from my soul, and for the first time since my painful breakup with Caleb, I didn't hate the sound of my own voice. I sang along, my voice harmonizing with the piano, creating a hauntingly beautiful tune that reverberated through the room.

The song was my secret, my confession, a testament to the emotions I couldn't voice aloud. The world outside ceased to exist, and I let myself be consumed by the raw emotion that poured from my heart.

When I finally came down from my musical high, I sighed with contentment, a small smile playing on my lips. I knew Cookie would love the song when I shared it with her, and she'd probably freak out when she heard the story behind it.

Someone cleared their throat. Startled, I glanced up and gasped softly when I saw Manny leaning against the door frame, his arms crossed casually. He wore a crisp white shirt that clung to his muscular frame, paired with black sweatpants that showcased the strength in his legs.

Caleb had always been lean and wiry, but Manny was different. He was solid, all muscle. My heart raced as he spoke, his voice breaking the silence.

"That was a nice song," he said, his tone warm.

I smiled. "Thank you."

Without hesitation, Manny grabbed a stool from my vanity table and moved to sit next to me behind the piano. The closeness between us was electrifying.

"Elena," he said. "You really love making music, don't you?"

I nodded, my fingers lightly tracing the smooth ivory keys of the piano. "It's my love. I've always found it easier to let my emotions go through music."

There was a fleeting, unreadable expression in Manny's eyes as he glanced between me and the piano. "Your voice was beautiful," he said.

A blush crept up my cheeks as I whispered another "thank you."

"Can I hear it again?" He asked.

My eyes widened. "You want to hear the same song?" I asked, my voice quivering slightly.

Manny shrugged, leaning in closer. "Any song, honestly. You can sing the ABC song for all I care. I just want to hear your voice."

My heart raced as I hesitated for a moment, then placed my hand on the piano keys. "This is the first song I ever wrote," I admitted, my voice trembling. "Maybe I'll tell you the story behind it after."

A warm smile spread across Manny's face, and he nodded. "That would be lovely."

I began to sing and my gaze was locked with Manny's. I couldn't look away. His unwavering attention, the intensity in his eyes, made it feel as though I was singing just for him. The connection between us in that moment was undeniable, and my heart swelled with a mixture of emotions, including a growing attraction that I could no longer deny.

CHAPTER NINE
MANNY

I watched Elena move gracefully around the cabin, humming a song that seemed to fill the air with an indescribable beauty. It had been two days since I'd heard her sing, and I found myself yearning for it, as if it scratched an itch deep within me. Her voice was more than just beautiful; there was something about it that stirred emotions I hadn't felt in a long time.

Or maybe it was just her.

As she walked past me, her humming faded into a soft tune. I watched her pick up two cushions to arrange them on the couch. Then I reached out and gently touched her shoulder. "Let me do that," I offered, my voice slightly husky.

She turned her head to look at me. "Okay, thanks, Manny!" she replied with a warm smile, her words causing a pleasant shiver to run down my spine.

Her voice was like a caress to my ears. I wanted to hear her say my name again, but in a different context. The thought of her gasping my name had my heart racing, and I had to take a deep breath to steady myself as she walked away from me.

I had tried to convince myself that Elena and I were too different, that we came from separate worlds, the night we got drunk and played that Scrabble game. But my attraction to her had only intensified since then, making it impossible to ignore the urge to touch her, to be close to her whenever she was around.

I stole a moment to glance outside the cabin window, where the forest lay bathed in the soft illumination of the night. The snow wasn't so frenzied anymore, and now everything was still. The trees stood tall and elegant, their branches adorned with a gentle layer of snowflakes. It was a serene, almost magical sight, and for a moment, I allowed myself to get lost in its beauty.

Then I heard Elena's hums again.

I ran a hand through my hair. Being around her was anything but safe for me. She was like a whirlwind of emotions and desires that I couldn't afford to entertain.

By the time I finished arranging the cushions, I knew I had to keep my distance. Tomorrow, if the weather held, I would get out of this cabin. I'd call Bethany, let her remind me of what was waiting for me back in the real world, and hopefully, she'd help me forget about the woman with forest-green eyes.

As I made my way over to the kitchen, the scent of something delicious wafting through the air, I found Elena at the stove, working on our dinner. She glanced over at me and smiled, her eyes filled with warmth. "Dinner will be ready soon," she informed me.

I nodded, before settling into a chair at the small dining table in the corner of the kitchen.

My gaze remained fixed on her as she gracefully moved about the kitchen. Then it shifted to an open book which was sitting on the table. I didn't think twice before reaching for it, my curiosity getting the best of me.

My eyes settled on the lyrics that adorned the page. It didn't take long to recognize them; they were the same lyrics Elena had sung while she played the piano, her voice dripping with beautiful melancholy.

"Your eyes held a promise, a future untold,
In your arms, I found the warmth to my cold.
In this tangled web of feelings, I'll always remember..."

A frown creased my brow as I read through her words. They were heartbreaking. Honestly, I could tell when I first heard them. And I would have been worried if I didn't see her smile when she was done singing like she had enjoyed every single second of it.

It was evident that these lyrics were born from a place of pain and heartache. It struck me then, like a bolt of lightning — these lyrics were about her ex-boyfriend.

My jaw clenched instinctively and there was that familiar burn in my chest when I remembered Elena had an ex-boyfriend. I was jealous, like a fucking high school kid. She just got out of a relationship and she was probably taking her time to grieve, and I wanted to rip the memory of him out of her head so she didn't think about him again.

I pushed the book away. What kind of thought was that?

My gaze snapped up to Elena just as she began to sing those same heart-wrenching words softly, her voice carrying a hint of sadness that I couldn't ignore.

"In the shadows of longing, I dared to dream,
But reality's cruel, tearing at the seam."

Of course, she still thought about him. How could she not? I didn't know much about their relationship but if they were in one, it must have hurt when they broke up.

Elena's voice broke through my thoughts, snapping me back to the present. "Dinner's ready!" she chimed, a cheerful note in her voice.

***

As I sat at the dining table, my appetite vanished into thin air. The aroma of the meal Elena had prepared wafted through the air, but my mind was preoccupied. I couldn't shake the thought that she still had feelings for her ex. It wasn't any of my business, so why did it feel so heavy?

My fork toyed idly with the pasta on my plate. Then I noticed from the corner of my eye that she was watching me, so I took a quick bite of the food. The pasta tasted exquisite, but my appetite had abandoned me. I took another small bite and washed it down with a generous gulp of water, trying to quell the unsettling feelings stirring within me.

"Manny?" Elena called and I turned to her with a raised brow. Her concerned gaze bore into me as she asked, "What's wrong?"

I hesitated, my eyes darting away from hers. How could I possibly tell her what was bothering me? That it was the idea of her still holding onto someone else, someone who wasn't me.

I muttered, "Nothing, I'm fine."

Elena let out a nervous chuckle. "Is the food bad?" She asked, "Or do you not like pasta?"

I mustered a weak smile. "The food is great as usual, Elena," I tried to say in a casual tone. But it came out flat.

My gaze flickered to the closed notebook sitting next to Elena's cup. It seemed to mock me, for thinking that a kid like me could ever be anything to a woman like her.

"I'm just not hungry," I said as I pushed my chair back abruptly and stood up. Without another word, I left the kitchen, walking away from Elena.

Stepping out into the living room, I quickly grabbed my jacket, determined to put some distance between myself and her. The frigid air hit me as I made my way outside, instantly sending shivers across my skin. The cold was like a slap in the face, but it was a welcome change from the stifling atmosphere inside.

I gazed up at the night sky, the stars glinting like distant diamonds. It was a clear night, and the tranquility of the forest was both eerie and comforting. Despite the crisp air, I couldn't shake the warmth her memory still lit up in me. I wished I could call Captain Rodriguez. He'd likely tell me that it seemed like I liked Elena, really liked her. And then he's said I should never call him this late again because evening time was for Emily, his wife.

I let out a frustrated groan. This situation was ridiculous. I couldn't afford to have feelings for someone so out of my league – a famous, older woman, hung up on her probably celebrity boyfriend.

"Manny?"

My body stiffened, and I turned to see Elena standing there, wrapped up in a puffy jacket with a hoodie pulled over her head. Even in the dim light, her face was visible, and as she exhaled, misty white puffs of breath escaped her mouth.

She was so beautiful.

"What's wrong?" she asked, concern etched into her features.

I tried to shrug off the tension that had settled over me like a heavy shroud, but I couldn't meet her gaze. "Nothing," I muttered. "You should go back inside."

Elena shook her head, her voice firm. "No, something's bothering you. You can talk to me if something happened."

How could I tell her that she was the reason? That it was her presence, her beauty, her kindness that had stirred emotions I couldn't control? I couldn't admit that to her.

I continued to evade her gaze, refusing to answer.

"Did I do something?" She asked.

In the quiet of my mind, I couldn't deny it. If she hadn't kissed me, if I hadn't come to the cabin, if I hadn't allowed myself to be drawn into this situation, I wouldn't be feeling so helpless.

I simply muttered, "Please, Elena, just go inside," I simply muttered. The night air was crisp and biting my skin as I added, "You'll catch a cold."

I watched as she glanced back at the cabin before turning her frown towards me. It was a look I hadn't seen on her before, and it caught me off guard. "You know, Manny? I'll never understand you," she said in a frustrated voice. "I could have understood why you didn't like me much in the beginning, but I thought we were... I thought maybe we could be..."

"We could be what?" I interrupted, searching her eyes for answers.

Elena hesitated, her gaze drifting away from mine, "Never mind," she mumbled.

I closed the distance between us and insisted, "Speak up. What did you think we could be?"

She took a deep breath and her frown deepened. "I thought we were at least better! That maybe we could be friends!" She raised her voice and yelled.

Her words hit me like a punch to the gut, and an involuntary sneer crossed my face. "Fuck that, Elena. I don't want to be your friend." I retorted sharply.

The very idea of being just her friend filled me with an inexplicable anger.

She placed her palm against my chest and pushed me forward. "Well, I don't want to be your friend either," she shot back, her frustration evident. "All I've done is be nice to you, but you're so avoidant, it's insane."

She moved forward to push me again but lost her footing on the snowy ground. I moved to catch her as she fell, but the world seemed to spin in slow motion as we both tumbled to the ground, with Elena landing on top of me. The unexpected physical contact sent a jolt of electricity through me, and for a moment, I forgot about everything else, lost in the sensation of her body pressed against mine.

I found myself staring into Elena's angry eyes, but I couldn't bring myself to be angry anymore, not when she was so close, her presence almost overwhelming amidst the cold.

With a teasing grin, I remarked, "You're so clumsy, always falling."

Elena frowned. "I tripped," she retorted, her voice laced with defiance. "If you hate it so much, maybe you shouldn't have caught me."

Her words hung in the air for a moment, and it felt like the world around us had disappeared. I couldn't look away from her. "I'll catch you," I said, my gaze dropping to her lips. "Every time you fall, I'll catch you."

My eyes met hers again, and without waiting for her reaction, I kissed her fiercely, passionately. The harshness of the kiss surprised us both as I sat up, pulling her with me until she was straddling my lap. Elena responded eagerly, and for a moment, time seemed to stand still. Her fingers found their way into my hair and I thought, "She wants this. She wants me."

I remembered the kiss from the day we met. This one was different. It wasn't the thrilling, heart-pounding moment of our first encounter. Instead, it was warm and sensual, sending tingles down my body, igniting a fire within me that I hadn't known before. As our lips moved together, I couldn't help but think, this kiss might just ruin me.

CHAPTER TEN

ELENA

What's happening?

Manny swept me off my feet, quite literally, as he slammed open the cabin door and shut it behind us. My mind was in a whirlwind, unable to fully comprehend what was happening. But deep down, I didn't want to think too much about it.

He carried me over to the couch, his gaze locked onto mine with an intensity that sent shivers down my spine. In that moment, I didn't care about explanations or uncertainties. What mattered was that Manny had kissed me, and it was a clear sign that he wanted me as much as I wanted him.

I put my hand on the side of his head, pulling it towards me. Then I kissed him long and hard. Manny's tongue flicked against mine and I realized that the kiss from the night we met had been nothing. This one was demanding, and hungry.

He placed one hand beside my head to brace himself while the other grazed the pants I wore. He moved it up and down the soft fabric, sending heat through my body.

I ran my fingers through his hair, applying pressure as his hand slowly moved from my thigh to rub my pussy through my panties. I broke away from the kiss and he placed his head on my shoulder, taking a deep breath.

"Oh God," I whimpered when he pressed against me through the fabric. He continued to rub faster and I could tell I was getting even wetter by the minute.

I leaned over and he moved his arms from my side to my back, lifting me quickly. He moved to sit and placed me on one leg, gripping my ass through my pants.

I moaned as he kissed me again and lightly squeezed my ass. Then he released me and said softly, "I need your clothes off, Elena."

I loved it when he said my name.

I felt hot in the clothes, so hot that I didn't mind Manny's gaze as I slipped out of the hoodie and everything else until I was wearing just underwear. He ran his fingers across my flesh, drawing lines over my thighs. One hand rose up over my bra strap to my shoulders.

Manny stared at me like he was contemplating what to do next and I felt vulnerable under his gaze. What did he see when he stared at me. His eyes moved to my face and they seemed to soften. "What's on your mind, Elena?" He asked.

"Why were you so mad at dinner?" I asked.

He moved his hand up, feeling the underside of my left breast first then completely engulfing it in his hand through my bra.

"Oh, yeah," I said softly.

The bra felt thin and tight against my skin, my nipples pushing against it. Manny reached inside the opening and could feel the top of my breast. "I was mad because..." He leaned in and kissed my cheek and neck, "...because I want you."

I gasped as he pushed his hand inside and underneath the bra, cupping my breast and squeezing my nipple gently. "W-why would that..."

"Make me mad?" He asked as his toyed with both my nipples in my bra. "Because I didn't think you wanted me, Elena."

I gasped and moaned softly as he played with my tits and my hand rode down his side, to his hip and onto his crotch. I could feel his cock hardening under his jeans and I rubbed over it.

"But I do want you, Manny," I said, my hips grinding against his thigh.

He inhaled sharply. "I can feel that," he said. "You're so wet for me."

I continued to play with him through his pants and he moved the strap of my bra over my shoulder. His fingers unhooked them from behind easily and he lean in to lick from my neck to the top of my breast and then to my nipple.

"Yes. Oh, Manny," I cried, pulling his head harder onto my breast. He sucked furiously, pushing my tits up with his hand. "Take your clothes off," I begged.

I reached for his shirt and began undoing the buttons. As he took it off, revealing his chiseled chest and sculpted muscles, I couldn't help but stare. My breath caught in my throat as my eyes traced the contours of his body, and a flush of desire crept up my cheeks. It was the first time I had seen him shirtless, and it left me utterly captivated.

Manny sat back and watched me, his bottom lip between his teeth. I wasted no time unfastening his belt and pulling down the zipper of his pants before taking the pants off. Then I inserted a hand into his boxer and found his rigid cock. My eyes widened as I pulled it out. I swallowed.

Manny is...big.

"Like what you see, sweetheart?" Manny asked as he managed to get his mouth onto one of my tits. He released it momentarily and said, "Don't let go," before he bit a nipple. "Touch me, Elena."

The more he sucked, the harder I squeezed. His right hand found its way back to my legs, only this time he moved up and straight to my pussy. He slipped his hand into my pants, reaching down until he found my clit. I inhaled sharply as he rubbed it.

"You're so wet, fuck," he said as he continued to tease me.

"I want you in me, Manny," I moaned. "Please."

He slipped his hand out of my panties and moved me off his lap. Then he placed me on the couch and got on his knees, shuffling down to my legs. He kissed my knee and then my thighs as he pulled off my panties.

I was now naked in front of him and his gaze met mine as he placed another kiss on my thigh. "You're so gorgeous," he said.

I bit my bottom lip, watching him as I spread my legs invitingly. He was gorgeous on his knees with his hair ruffled and his eyes shining with pure lust.

"I have a question," he said and I groaned.

"Not now," I said as his hands moved up outside my thighs.

"You're going to have to answer me."

His head was directly on my pussy and I couldn't help but be glad that I had shaved recently. He rubbed against my clit.

"Do you still love him?" He asked.

Huh?

What was he talking about?

He slipped a finger into me and then another. "Answer me, Elena."

"W-who?" I asked before tipping my head back and moaning.

"Your ex."

I dropped my head to stare at him. Was he seriously thinking about Caleb at a time like this? He wasn't supposed to be thinking of anything besides me. "Of course not, are you crazy?"

Manny grinned, playfully and that seemed to be enough of a response for him because his tongue quickly found the opening between my pussy lips and I stiffened.

"Oh, fuck. Ah..."

He put his hands under my ass and lifted me into his mouth. He moved until he found my clit with his tongue and surrounded it with his lips. My body shook as he nibbled on it.

"Yes, there. Yes," I said.

It didn't take long for me to feel an orgasm building up within me. I was going to cum. But then Manny slid up farther and kissed me, slipping his tongue into my mouth so I could taste myself.

"You taste so good, Elena," He said, "But when you cum, it's going to be around my cock."

He placed the tip of his cock at the entrance to my pussy. He slid in easily and as soon as I wrapped my legs around his waist, he pushed until our bodies met.

"Fuck, Elena," He groaned.

"Fuck me please," I whined desperately.

The feeling of Manny's cock inside me sent shivers through me each time he thrusted. He was slow, gentle at first and I wanted it to last forever. I looked down to see him sliding in and out of me, the sheer size shocking me again. I couldn't believe I was even taking him, and it felt so good.

I felt like I was going to cum again.

Manny held onto my ass with both hands and continued to thrust into me. I moaned louder as he slid in and out. My breasts bounced, my legs widened and I felt my body begin to shake.

"God, I'm gonna cum," I said.

"Let go sweetheart," he said and that was all I needed.

I exhaled deeply and groaned. My hips rose and fell uncontrollably as I came and Manny continued to fuck me through it. I wrapped my arms around his neck and brought his lips to mine.

Muffled grunts and groans came from Manny's lips as wave after wave of orgasm hit me. He bit my lip and I gasped. "You're so beautiful," He said, "You make me want to cum."

"Inside me please," I said. I wasn't even sure where the thought came from. I was on the pill so it was safe but I didn't think about that. I just wanted to feel him spill inside me.

I felt it moments later and Manny pulled me up by the ass, thrusting into me as he came, curses falling from his lips. He pumped me with his cum over and over again and I moaned, tightening my thighs around his waist.

Finally, he collapsed on the couch next to me. Then he moved to kiss me and it was slow, sensual, going on for what seemed like forever.

I didn't have the words when he released me but he did. "That was amazing, Elena," he said and I smiled.

It was more than amazing.

***

Manny and I were cuddled up under a cozy blanket in my room. He cradled my face gently in his large, warm hands, and I relished the feeling of his touch. His eyes, so deep and expressive, were fixed on mine.

He glanced over at the piano sitting in the corner of my room and his voice was soft as he asked, "Do all your songs have special meanings for you?"

I nodded, hesitating for a moment.

"What about the new song you wrote?"

My heart raced. I wondered if I should tell him that it was about him. What if he thought it was strange, writing a song about someone so quickly? What if, for him, this wasn't more than sex.

"It's fine if it's about that Caleb guy," he said, his jaw clenching.

My eyes widened in surprise, and I quickly shook my head. "No," I said, my voice barely a whisper. "It's not about Caleb. It's about you."

His frown turned into a look of astonishment, and then his eyes lit up. "Oh," he said, his voice filled with relief. "Well, that feels better."

I tilted my head, a teasing smile forming on my lips. "Were you jealous?" I asked playfully.

He rolled his eyes in response but didn't deny it. Instead, he leaned in and kissed me, and all doubts and uncertainties seemed to melt away in that moment.

CHAPTER ELEVEN
MANNY

I walked towards the fire station with a mixture of relief and reluctance. The storm had finally subsided enough for Elena and me to leave the cabin, and even though I knew it was coming, I couldn't help feeling a pang of sadness.

I missed her.

Elena and I had left together in my car yesterday. And I hadn't spoken to her since I dropped her off. She collected my number and said she would text me.

I paused in front of the station and stared at my phone.

Still nothing.

Did our time together mean nothing?

I shoved my phone into my pocket and ran my fingers through my hair. Maybe she had gone back to her life as an award-winning musician and forgotten about the amazing sex we had. No, that was impossible. I was simply unforgettable.

I needed to be patient. I mean, she was a busy woman which was fine. I was a busy man too. I walked into the fire station with a plastered grin on my face. "Hey, I'm back!" I announced to everyone as I entered. They all paused in their various activities and turned to look at me. Liam, one of the guys, furrowed his brow. "Back from where?"

I chuckled. "I've been stuck in a cabin in the woods, guys. Sent a text to Omar."

Just as I mentioned Omar, he walked out of the captain's office and, upon seeing me, his expression shifted from confusion to mild irritation. "You're alive?"

I furrowed my brows at him. "What's that supposed to mean?" I asked. "I sent a text. You read it."

A sound came from his phone and he slipped it out of his pocket as he stared at me. "Yeah, I read your text but you took too long to come back that I thought the worst. I was preparing for your funeral."

I grimaced. "Are you serious man?"

Omar flashed a grin. "Of course not," he said before glancing at his phone. "Jenn is calling. Go wash your fucking gear."

He walked away, leaving me dumbfounded. "I just got back!" I said.

"And?" Mel, one of the firefighters said as she walked past me. "You thought we'd do it for you?"

I sighed as I moved towards a bench and sat. I dropped my bag next to me and was about to check my phone when it chimed with a message from an unknown number. My heart skipped a beat as I saw her text, even before she confirmed her identity. Elena's message was a simple *"hey"* with a heart emoji that brought a smile to my face.

"Took you long enough," I responded.

She sent a laughing emoji and then, *"I'm sorry. I've been busy."*

"You're going to have to make it up to me."

"How?"

I swallowed hard as my thumb moved across the screen. *"Preferably with your mouth wrapped around my..."*

"We have an emergency!" Omar's voice boomed, distracting me. "Get ready!"

I hurriedly grabbed my bag, ready to spring into action.

My phone chimed again, and I glanced at the screen to see another message from Elena. *"What are you doing on Friday?"*

I grinned. *"Depends..."*

"On what?"

"On whether I get to see you or not."

She responded with a laughing emoji, which warmed my heart. Her next message brought a smile to my face. *"You'll get to see me."*

"Then I guess I'm free."

"I'll send you the address soon."

Despite the impending firefighting mission, the thought of seeing Elena again filled me with excitement and anticipation. Friday couldn't come any faster.

Later that evening, I found myself nervously dialing Elena's number. When she answered with that soft, melodic "Hello," my chest warmed, and I felt a rush of relief.

"Hey," I managed to say, though I wasn't entirely sure what to say next.

"Hi," she replied, and it was awkward, but in a strangely comforting way.

I collapsed on my bed... "So, what's happening on Friday?" I asked.

"It's my first performance in a while," She confessed.

"And how does that make you feel?"

There was a brief pause before she said, "Hesitant. Not all the recent media attention has been positive. For example, did you know some people think you're a gigolo?"

I sat up. "What? Where did that come from?"

She laughed out loud and I wanted to bottle up the sound. "I don't know Manny. People are absurd," she said. "It's funny, isn't it? No one's even suggested that you might be my boyfriend. Probably because of the age difference. They're likely wondering what someone like you would see in someone like me."

The words hung in the air, and I could sense the uncertainty in her tone. I thought it was funny that she wondered about that because I wondered if she actually wanted me too.

I cleared my throat. "Elena, I'd want to have so much with someone like you, if you'd let me."

Her sharp intake of breath on the other end sent a thrill through me. Then, in a soft voice, she admitted, "I miss you."

"I miss you too," I replied.

***

I made my way to the grand hotel, the imposing architecture leaving me feeling somewhat insignificant. As I walked up the entrance, I handed the doorman the entry pass Elena had sent me the day before. He scrutinized me briefly before granting me access with a nod. I took a deep breath before I walked in.

"Here we go," I muttered as I took out my phone and sent Elena a message to let her know I had arrived. The hotel lobby was bustling with people, all dressed in their designer clothes, giving off an air of sophistication that made me feel a bit out of place.

Another impeccably dressed gentleman, dressed in black, walked up to me. "Good day sir, are you here for the wine party?" He asked.

I blinked at him before nodding in response and he gestured for me to follow him. I shoved my hands into my pockets and followed.

He led me into a vast ballroom that was nothing short of grandiose. The room was bathed in a soft, romantic glow, the only light coming from an array of crystal chandeliers that hung from the ceiling like stars in the night sky. Their shimmering reflections danced across the polished marble floor, creating an illusion of a thousand constellations beneath my feet.

The walls were adorned with intricate, gold-trimmed moldings, and large windows framed with heavy drapes allowed the moonlight to filter through, casting long shadows that added an air of mystery. The soft, soothing notes of a grand piano filled the air, lending an elegant soundtrack to the evening.

A waiter approached me with a glass of wine, which I accepted and tried to sip slowly. It tasted so good I wanted to drink it all but I wasn't sure how that would make me look. I scanned the room, searching for a glimpse of Elena. My phone remained silent, and I wondered why she hadn't replied yet.

I sighed, shoving my hand into my pocket, and settled for sipping my champagne, hoping that she would show up soon. A few seconds later, I noticed a man walking up to me, a grim look on his face.

"Good evening," he said.

"Good evening," I gave him a curt nod.

"And who might you be sir?"

"Manuel Delgado," I answered. "I'm a friend of Elena Foster."

The stranger regarded me for a moment longer before finally speaking. "Manuel Delgado, you say? A friend of Elena's?"

I nodded, my gaze sweeping the hall briefly before it returned back to him. "Yes, that's right."

He seemed to deliberate over my response, and then, with a hint of curiosity, he asked, "How exactly did you meet Elena?"

I furrowed my brows and he arched an eyebrow, scrutinizing me in a way that made me slightly uncomfortable. He looked sophisticated, and the watch on his wrist alone was probably worth more than my car.

Before I could respond, the curtains at the end of the hall gracefully slid open, revealing a beautifully decorated stage. My breath caught in my throat as I laid eyes on Elena for the first time that evening.

Or since we left the cabin.

She was a vision in a long, green dress that seemed to mirror the depths of her forest-green eyes. Her hair, elegantly swept up and pinned at the back, showcased the graceful curve of her neck. She looked utterly enchanting, and for a moment, the rest of the world faded away as I found myself captivated by her presence.

As Elena took the stage, I couldn't help but feel a surge of pride and anticipation. "Thank you all so much for being here tonight. I hope you're enjoying the evening. It means the world to me to have you here."

The crowd responded with applause and cheers before she continued. "I would like to begin our night with a song that's very special to me. It's a song I recently wrote, dedicated to someone who has grown on me and found a unique place in my heart."

She cast her gaze across the audience, and when her eyes found mine, she gifted me with a smile that made my heart skip a beat.

However, her smile quickly faded as her gaze shifted next to me, and she faltered briefly. I followed her line of sight and saw a man staring at her with a clenched jaw. What the hell was his deal?

Before I could dwell on it too long, Elena looked away and smiled again. "I hope you enjoy this song as much as I enjoyed creating it," she said.

Then she began to sing.

Elena's voice was captivating, carrying a depth of emotion that resonated throughout the room. It was the same song she'd written while we were in the cabin, and hearing her perform it in this grand setting gave it a whole new dimension. As she sang, it was as if the entire room fell under her spell. Or maybe it was just me, because I couldn't notice anyone else anyway. Her passion and talent were undeniable, and I couldn't tear my eyes away from her.

Elena's song seemed to transcend the boundaries of the room, connecting us in a way that words couldn't express. It was a beautiful and intimate performance. And it was for me. She was singing the song she wrote for me.

As the song ended, the room exploded with cheers and applause. The sound of their clapping and the excitement in the air was electric. But Elena's gaze remained locked on me. Her eyes sparkled with a triumphant grin, and in that moment, it felt like there was no one else in the room but us. I couldn't help but return her smile, beaming with pride.

As she walked down from the stage, my eyes followed her every move. I watched as she made her way through the crowd, receiving compliments and praise from the guests. My fingers wrapped around the champagne flute in my hand, and I downed the remaining liquid in one swift gulp.

The man who had been standing next to me earlier excused himself and walked away. I was going to ask Elena who he was after I had her close to me again, after I held her in my arms, and kissed her...a lot.

Our eyes locked again and she tilted her head ever so discreetly toward the side of the hall. It was all the signal I needed, and a grin crept onto my face.

I slipped through the crowd, feeling the anticipation building with each step toward the exit. Once outside, I found a spiral staircase, leading upward. Without hesitation, I climbing, each step bringing me closer to the small balcony that overlooked Baileys Harbor.

The view that met my eyes was nothing short of breathtaking. The town sparkled beneath the dark velvet of the night sky, its lights shimmering like stars on Earth. The harbor waters glistened with reflections of the moon, creating a serene ambiance.

I didn't immediately notice the approaching footsteps. But when I did, I turned to find Elena climbing the stairs. Our gazes met, and a genuine smile graced my lips. "Hello, star," I greeted, stretching my hand out to her.

She took my hand. "Why 'star'?"

I pulled her closer, the distance between us quickly closing. "Because that's what you looked like tonight," I confessed, my voice low. "So bright and beautiful that I couldn't keep my eyes off you."

She chuckled, a warm, melodic sound that filled the night air. As I held her in my arms, the world around us seemed to disappear, leaving only the two of us.

"You're so cheesy," she said.

"Only with you," I replied, just before I leaned in and kissed her lightly on the lips.

The kiss was soft, almost tentative, yet filled with an underlying intensity that neither of us could deny. I tasted the sweetness of her lips, and my heart raced as our mouths moved together, each fleeting touch sending shivers down my spine. My hand found its way to the nape of her neck, my fingers tangling in her hair as I held her close.

When I finally pulled away, I found myself lost in her gaze, her forest-green eyes holding a spell over me. I took a deep breath. I had been with a lot of women, so many that it may scare her away but my heart was never pounding around them the way it was at this moment.

"What did you mean when you said you want to have so much to do with me?" She asked.

I tilted my head, a small smile playing on my lips. "I want a lot of things," I admitted, my voice low and intimate. "But what do you want, Star?"

She blinked, her teeth grazing her bottom lip in a gesture that sent a surge of desire through me. I swallowed...hard, fighting the urge to kiss her again.

"I'm not sure," She said in a hesitant tone, "I just know I want something more meaningful than a casual fling."

"I haven't had anything more meaningful than a casual fling since high school," I said.

Her eyes widened. "So, you're a whore?"

I leaned back and laughed. "Who still says whore these days?" I asked.

She rolled her eyes and looked away from me.

Gently, I cradled her chin in my hand, and moved her head so she was staring at me again. "I want something more too but we don't have to hurry if you're not sure," I said. "When you're ready, just let me know. We can be so much more, Elena."

She exhaled deeply and smiled. "Okay," she said softly.

"Okay," I said, before I kissed her again.

CHAPTER TWELVE
ELENA

I stared at the pile of papers Cookie had just handed me, my heart pounding in my chest. The words on those documents seemed almost surreal, like a dark fantasy I couldn't escape. While I had been secluded at the cabin, disconnected from the world, Cookie had been working tirelessly to uncover a truth.

"How did you find out all of this?" I finally managed to ask, my voice trembling with a mixture of anger and disbelief.

She leaned forward, her eyes locked onto mine, her expression grave. "When I let Eugene go," she began, "I told him I'd report him and get his bodyguard license revoked. He... he cracked, Elena."

I clenched my jaw, my stomach churning with a cocktail of emotions. "And?" I urged.

"He spilled everything," Cookie said. "Eugene told me that Caleb introduced him to a reporter named Felix from New York. Since Caleb lost his influence over you, Eugene started feeding Felix information."

The weight of those words hung heavy in the air. Cookie got suspicious when she found out about this, so she started to investigate.

Caleb had not only been the source of the rumors that tainted my reputation but he also mismanaged my finances and exploited me.

My blood boiled.

"I have to get rid of him," I said.

Cookie nodded. "If you want, we'll take legal action Elena. We'll make sure he pays for what he's done."

I stared at the papers spread out before me. It was time to take control of my life once and for all. "Call the lawyer," I said.

The next few days were a whirlwind of legal consultations, meetings, and strategizing on how to confront Caleb. It was a battle I was determined to win, not just for myself but for my career and reputation.

A few days later, I was in the studio, recording the song inspired by Manny. Tony, my friend and producer grinned as I belted out the lyrics, the music filling the studio.

"Elena, you sound amazing!" He clapped his hands and said. "Wanna take a break?"

I smiled. "Thanks Tony," I said, "Sure, let's take a break."

As I grabbed a bottle of water and checked my phone, Manny's message popped up. Manny loved to send memes and they never failed to make me smile. I was in the middle of typing a response when I heard a voice.

"Elena?"

My heart sank as I looked up to see Caleb standing in the studio doorway.

I walked out of the recording studio, my heart racing and he moved out of the way. Then he met me in the hallway.

"Caleb," I said. "What are you doing here?"

Caleb didn't look the least bit surprised to see me. "I'm your manager, Elena. I don't need an invitation."

I let out a humorless laugh, my voice dripping with sarcasm. "Didn't you hear from the lawyer?"

His expression remained unperturbed. "I don't care about any lawyer. I care about you."

I sighed, the tension in the air palpable. "Why am I not surprised?"

His voice softened as he took a step closer. "Elena, are you really doing this? Is this all just revenge for what you found out about me and that woman?"

I shook my head, feeling a strange mix of emotions at the memory. "No. It's not about that anymore. I would have been fine with you as my manager despite our personal issues, but you betrayed me."

"I would never betray you, Elena. You know me. We've been together for years."

Memories of our journey together flashed through my mind. How Caleb had secured my first record deal, how he had been the one to push me to perform in public when I was just starting out. It was undeniable that he had played a significant role in my career.

But it turned out I did not know him at all.

"I am grateful for everything you've done for me," I admitted, my voice softer. "But are you really going to deny stealing from me and spreading rumors about me?"

The air between us crackled with tension. I stared at Caleb, waiting for his response, my gaze roaming over the man I had once thought would be by my side forever. He was still as striking as ever, his perfectly groomed appearance masking the person beneath the surface. His deep-set eyes that used to make me feel warm inside now only filled me with a sense of resentment.

His jaw clenched as he met my gaze, his voice laced with bitterness. "Were they even rumors, Elena? I saw the fireman you kissed at your performance the other day."

I frowned, recalling how I had seen Caleb standing beside Manny during my performance. I didn't get a chance to ask Manny if they talked and what they talked about.

"How am I even sure you weren't cheating on me?" Caleb asked.

I grimaced. The audacity of this man.

"I would never stoop so low as to cheat on you, Caleb," I snapped back in a firm voice. "I'm not the disgusting person you've become."

The words hung in the air between us, and I took deep breath. I wasn't going to let him manipulate me anymore.

"I don't care what you say," I declared, "Whatever happened between us is over. Not only is what I have with Manny none of your business, but you're no longer my manager. I'm going to make sure you pay for trying to ruin me."

I moved to walk past Caleb, determined to leave him alone and put this chapter of my life behind me. But he grabbed my arm, halting my steps, and his voice wavered with desperation.

"I'm sorry, Elena," he murmured, his words laced with regret. "I made a mistake. That woman, it was my first time. She came onto me, and I'm so sorry."

His eyes bore into mine, pleading for forgiveness, and I couldn't help but frown in disbelief. He was still trying to lie to me?

I quickly pulled my arm out of his grip, my voice tinged with anger. "It wasn't your first time," I retorted, my voice trembling with anger. "I saw your phone, Caleb. I know that woman you were with wasn't the first, so don't even try to deny it."

He remained silent.

"You're pathetic," I spat. "If you have anything to say to me in the future, I suggest you communicate through my lawyer."

When he didn't respond, I walked back into the studio. My phone chimed, and I saw a meme from Manny, one about a whale, and I chuckled before typing out a response.

"Elena," Tony called and I looked up. "You ready?" He asked.

I nodded, leaving Caleb and his silly apologies behind as I stepped back into the recording booth and let the music wash over me.

CHAPTER THIRTEEN
ELENA

I couldn't help but smile as a message lit up my phone screen. Jumping up from my chair, I saw Cookie watching me with a knowing glint in her eye.

"Is that Manny?" she asked with a grin.

I nodded. "Yes, it is! He just sent me his address."

Cookie raised one brow and a hint of mischief danced in her eyes. "You're going to his place?"

I nodded again. "Yup, but he doesn't know that. I told him I have a gift for him and a dispatch driver is dropping it off."

"But you're going by yourself."

I chuckled and leaned in closer. "I want to see the look on his face when he realizes," I whispered.

Cookie laughed. "You've been a lot more playful since this Manny guy came into your life."

I couldn't deny it. I thought so too. "You'll meet him soon, and I'm sure you'll love him."

With that, I left Cookie and headed to my room to get ready. Once I was prepared, I donned a beanie and a face mask. I didn't want to be recognized on my way to Manny's house and I wasn't so sure the paparazzi were off my back yet. I carefully tucked the gift I had gotten for Manny into a tote bag and then called an Uber.

As the Uber driver pulled up to Manny's house, I glanced at the building in mild surprise. I had expected an apartment building, but instead, there stood a charming townhouse. It was nestled between two other similar townhouses, and the neighborhood was quiet and serene.

The driver turned to me and announced, "We're here."

I paid him, then stepped out of the car, my tote bag clutched securely in my hand. I walked up to Manny's front door and knocked, but there was no immediate response. I knocked again, a bit more insistently this time.

He said he was going to be home today so where was he?

Finally, the door creaked open, revealing a woman. She was draped in a luxurious robe, her brunette hair falling gracefully around her shoulders. Her striking beauty could easily have graced the pages of a fashion magazine.

My eyes widened as I blinked at her, momentarily caught off guard.

The woman frowned as she scrutinized me. "Who the hell are you?" She asked, in a voice that held a note of suspicion.

I hesitated for a moment, casting a quick glance around the serene neighborhood. "I'm sorry," I replied, "but I'm looking for Manuel Delgado."

She continued to study me, from head to toe, before responding coldly, "He's not in right now." Her tone was curt. I didn't like it. "I'll ask again. Who are you?"

I could feel the tension in the air rise. "I'm... I'm a friend," I managed to say.

Her expression hardened as she fired back, "What kind of friend? Manny doesn't have female friends he's not fucking."

I blinked, feeling a pang of discomfort at her words. It was as if the ground had shifted beneath me, and I found myself on the defensive. Before I could respond, Manny's voice rang out from behind me, "What the fuck?"

I turned to face him with a mix of surprise and anxiety. And he frowned for a moment before recognition filled his features. His eyes softened. "Star?"

His gaze then shifted to the brunette woman and he rose a brow. "Beth? What are you doing here?"

The air grew thick with unspoken tension as my heart sank. Beth. Who was Beth?

My heart was pounding, and my mind was racing. I felt a growing urge to get out of this awkward situation. "I should probably leave," I said walking back to the road.

As I walked past Manny, he grabbed my elbow firmly.

"No," he said, his voice resolute, and pulled me toward the door.

"What are you doing here?" Manny asked Beth, his voice tinged with annoyance as he glanced back at her.

She explained, "I came to surprise you, Manny. You haven't been answering my calls."

His tone remained cold as he replied, "Well, you've seen me. Now, it's time for you to leave." He then guided me towards the door.

I followed him, feeling like an intruder in this situation.

As we entered the living room, Beth trailed behind us, seemingly unwilling to give up. "What the fuck Manny? I got your text," she said.

"If you got my text, why are you here?" He asked as he stopped in front of a couch.

"You can't just end things between us without an explanation!"

My gaze flitted between them, and the realization hit me like a ton of bricks: Manny was with her, or at least he used to be. His eyes met mine briefly, and I could sense his discomfort. I swallowed hard, feeling an uncomfortable mix of emotions. Beth was indeed beautiful, and my insecurities were flaring up.

He took a deep breath and turned to me, "I'm sorry, star. Please, have a seat on the couch and wait for me."

I nodded, and he left my side, walking towards Beth. He grasped her hand and led her away from the living room. As she followed, she glared at me.

I sat on the couch and crossed my legs. I heard the door shut which meant Manny had taken her outside. I strained to listen to their conversation from where I sat, my curiosity and anxiety growing.

Beth's wasted no time in demanding answers. "Who is the woman in there?" she asked, her tone sharp and accusatory.

Manny sighed deeply. "It's none of your business." He said.

She shot back. "You need to stop acting like a jerk, Manny. I deserve an explanation."

His voice remained firm. "We made a deal, Bethany," he said, "and I remember you saying that you owe me nothing. I agreed to that. But you've been calling since I sent that text and now you came here."

There was a heavy pause, and I held my breath, not wanting to miss a word.

Bethany's voice wavered as she admitted, "I know I said that but that was before."

Manny's response was gentle but resolute. "You can't just show up at my house whenever you feel like it." He added, "This is embarrassing."

"I'm sorry," she said.

"You need to leave."

Then came the question that hung in the air like a storm cloud, "Is there someone else?"

Manny's reply was simple but final, "You should go back home."

With that, I heard the door shut, and the tension that had filled the room seemed to dissipate. Manny was coming back, and I wasn't sure what I was going to say to him

He re-entered the living room, shrugging off his jacket with a fluid grace. My heart skipped a beat as I noticed the shirt he wore underneath, snugly hugging his well-defined muscles. It took a moment for me to realize he was watching me intently as he approached.

With deliberate care, he knelt before me and reached out, gently removing my beanie and face mask. A smile graced his lips as his warm gaze met mine, and my stomach did a nervous somersault.

"I'm sorry you had to see that, especially the first time you visited," he began, his voice soft and contrite.

I managed a faint smile, my voice playful. "We can have a re-do if you want. I can go to the front door and knock again, and you can answer this time."

He chuckled, a sound that sent a delightful shiver down my spine. "As tempting as that sounds, I think we'll save the re-do for another occasion."

I nodded, and he added, "I was surprised when I saw you."

"That's what I was hoping for," I said, "Though not the way it happened."

He studied me for a while before he spoke. "Bethany was a friend with benefits. We weren't in a relationship," He explained, "In fact, I haven't been in a relationship with anyone since high school."

His words hung in the air, and I tried to hide the relief I felt. "You don't have to explain, Manny," I offered gently.

Manny's gaze never left mine as he replied, "I know I don't have to, but I want to."

A warm smile tugged at my lips. "So, are there any more 'friends with benefits' I should be wary of?" I asked.

His chuckled, his eyes dancing with amusement. "I got rid of all of them," he assured me.

I let out a faux gasp. "How many were there?" I said.

Manny pretended to think for a second and then he said, "Well, there was Ashley, Cara..."

I playfully hit his shoulder. "That was a rhetorical question!"

He laughed and smoothly moved to sitting on the couch next to me. His proximity sent a thrilling shiver down my spine, and I felt a delicious warmth spreading through my chest. Manny's gaze remained intense as he continued, "Honestly, it doesn't matter how many there were. All I need is for you to say you're ready."

I raised an eyebrow, my heart pounding in my chest. "Ready for what?"

He smirked, a playful glint in his eyes. "To be my girlfriend."

A surge of emotions welled up within me as I considered his words. I hesitated, "Manny, have you really thought about our age difference?"

His expression turned serious for a moment, but then he shook his head slowly. "Elena, haven't you heard that age is just a number?" he asked.

His words melted away my reservations, and I blinked at him, my heart swelling. Manny didn't seem to care about our age gap, so why should I? Before I could say anything more, he closed the distance between us with a deep, passionate kiss, and I surrendered willingly.

The kiss deepened. Manny's arms encircled me, pulling me closer to him, and I could feel the pounding of his heart, echoing my own. The taste of him, the warmth of his mouth against mine, sent shivers coursing through my entire being.

Reluctantly, I pulled away, my breath coming in short, ragged gasps. My voice trembled as I stammered, "I... I got you a gift."

Manny's eyes bore into mine, his gaze smoldering with desire. He brushed a stray strand of hair from my face and whispered, "You can show it to me later. Right now, all I want is you. I missed you."

Without waiting for my response, he leaned in, capturing my lips in another searing kiss, erasing any doubts or worries that had lingered in my mind. In that moment, there was nothing, no Bethany, no worries about our age difference, just an overwhelming need for him that consumed me.

Manny leaned into me and I fell back on the couch. Then he pulled my shirt over my head. The cool air in the house caressed my bare skin and both my breasts throbbed.

A nervous shiver ran through me. I wasn't sure why I was nervous, especially when Manny reached into my bra and his fingers grazed my nipples.

I closed my eyes at the pleasure of his warm hands. "I...I'm not going to lie, I wasn't expecting you to live in a neighborhood like this," I said.

He chuckled. "The houses used to belong to my dad. He used to be a real estate investor," He explained. "Before he retired and left them to me."

I wasn't able to respond because he leaned in and press a kiss to the side of my neck.

"Do you know how often I think about fucking you?" He asked.

I shook my head and he kissed my cheek.

"Too many times in a day to count," he said.

I whimpered as he pulled off my jeans and then my panties quickly. He lay on top of me, spreading my legs open with his knees.

I heard him sigh as he took off the pants he was wearing. "If you want me to stop, say the word and I will," he said.

I shook my head and he groaned deeply as he pushed deep inside me. I arched my back, feeling sweat dampen my forehead and restrained breaths go through my lips.

"So...fucking...warm," Manny hissed.

My body responded like it remembered his. I brought my knees up either side of hips as he pushed his waist down against me.

"Fuck, Elena," He sighed, sliding in and out of me. My moans echoed through the living room as his hard cock stretched me out.

I ran my fingers through his hair. Then cupped his face. "You feel so good," I said.

Manny kept the rhythm with his hips. He was slow, sensual and gentle. He placed his arms on either side of my head so he was staring at me. I couldn't tell what the look in his eyes was but it was electrifying being the object of that gaze.

He lowered his mouth so he had my tits in his mouth. I writhed in pleasure under him as he sucked. A throbbing sensation went through me, all the way to my chest and I came around him.

Manny swallowed my scream with a kiss as he continued to fuck me through my orgasm and then he let out a loud, muffled groan as he pulled out and stroked his cock.

I moved quickly so I was on my knees and took it from him, feeling him throb in my palm. Then I wrapped my lips around him and sucked. "E...Elena..." Manny stuttered as his hips bucked and he came in my mouth.

I looked up at him, at the way he tipped his head back as he came and his lips parted. When he looked down at me, he ran his fingers through my hair and a wide grin formed on his face but that wasn't what was so beautiful at that moment. It was the fiery look in his eyes. I never wanted to forget how it made me feel.

Scratch that. I was never going to forget.

CHAPTER FOURTEEN
MANNY

I walked into the fire station with a grin. Next to me, Omar sighed tiredly. There was a fire at some old man's tap-dancing school and it was a pretty big one.

I loved it.

"Good job today, Samaritan!" I wrapped an arm around Omar's neck, playfully squeezing his shoulder.

His gaze moved to me and he chuckled, shaking his head. "You too, Manny."

I headed to the shower room. The day had been long, and the cool water felt refreshing against my skin. Thoughts of Elena had been racing through my mind all day, and now, without the distractions of work, they came flooding back.

I dressed quickly and sat down on a bench, picking up my phone. Still no response from her. I pouted slightly as I sent her another text, my fingers dancing across the screen.

"You haven't texted me back all day. I hope to God you are not ghosting me."

She liked me as much as I liked her. There was no way she was ghosting me.

Right?

Spending time with Elena had brought a kind of happiness I'd never known before. My heart would race when I was around her, and it was both exhilarating and terrifying. I didn't know the first thing about being in a relationship, but I knew I wanted Elena to be my girlfriend.

I ran my fingers through my hair, trying to make sense of these new feelings. Every time I saw her, or even just a picture of her, I felt this overwhelming desire to protect her, to protect her from the spotlight of fame. So, I was sure it wasn't just a casual fling; it was something deeper. It was a feeling I couldn't ignore, and it scared me a little.

No, I couldn't be scared. I'm Manny Delgado, and Manny Delgado fears nothing. When I started dating Elena, I was going to be the best boyfriend in the world. I'd treat her so right that she'd wonder why she ever dated anyone else. A smile crept onto my face as I thought about it.

But my reverie was suddenly shattered when Kelly, one of the workers at the fire station, burst out of the office in a dramatic frenzy, screaming at the top of her lungs. Omar groaned from where he stood.

"Please, Kelly, not now," he pleaded, rubbing his temples.

Kelly fell to her knees dramatically. "Not now?!" She yelled. "My idol has just been in an accident!"

I couldn't help but chuckle at the theatrical display. "Who's your idol, Kelly?" I asked casually, not really expecting an answer.

But Kelly's eyes widened, and she scuttled over to me like a spider on the prowl. She thrust her phone in my face, and I reluctantly took it, scrolling through the news article she had open.

"It's the woman you kissed, Manny!" She declared.

It was dated just a few minutes ago, and the headline sent a shock-wave through me. "Elena Foster in Accident."

I muttered to myself, "Is this real?" Kelly grabbed the phone back from me, her voice frantic, "Of course, it's real! TMZ never lies."

A ripple of murmurs passed through the fire station as the news spread, and my heart sank like a stone in my chest. Everything around me faded and all I could think about was Elena.

Elena had been in an accident.

Time seemed to blur as I grabbed my bag and sprinted out of the fire station. Ignoring the confused faces and murmurs of the people around me, I made a beeline for my car.

Once I was inside the car, I dialed Elena's number with trembling fingers. The phone rang incessantly and each second feeling like an eternity. My heart pounded in my chest as panic tightened its grip on me.

She didn't pick up.

Without wasting another moment, I started the engine and sped out of the fire station. It was late, and I knew I'd probably catch some heat from Omar for leaving before my shift ended. But none of that mattered—nothing except Elena.

Dialing her number again, I drove aimlessly, torn between heading to her house, her studio, or maybe even a hospital. I didn't even know where she was.

The call went through this time, and a brief sense of relief washed over me. Had she picked up? If she had, it meant she was okay. But the voice that came through was not Elena's.

"Hello?"

"Who is this?" I demanded, my voice shaking.

"Cookie," the woman said. "You're Manny. I was going to call you in a bit."

My heart sank further and questions tumbled out in a torrent, "Where's Elena? What happened?"

"You heard..." She trailed, "I don't really know the name of this hospital so I'll send you an address soon," she said in a shaky voice. "Please, get here quickly."

The sense of urgency in her voice was enough to send shivers down my spine. So, when the call came through, I raced towards the hospital, the darkness of the night seeming to close in around me.

***

I rushed into the hospital, my heart still pounding with anxiety. Once again, I called Elena's number, this time to let Cookie know that I had arrived. Then, I waited in the lobby, each passing second stretching into an agonizing eternity.

Finally, a voice called my name, and I turned to see her walking up to me. It was the first time I had met Elena's best friend in person. Elena had talked about her a lot, and under different circumstances, I would have been pleased to put a face to the name. But my joy was instantly extinguished when I saw Cookie's disheveled appearance—clothes in disarray, bloodshot eyes that spoke of tears, and her once-neat afro now a tangled mess.

My heart sank, and I could barely find my voice as I croaked, "Is she okay?"

She motioned for me to follow her, and I did, my mind reeling with fear.

As we walked through the hospital's sterile halls, Cookie explained what had happened. Elena had finished her session at the studio and was leaving when a drunk driver, out of nowhere, hit her

I stopped in my tracks. "Hit her?" I stammered.

Tears welled up in Cookie's eyes, and her voice quivered as she whispered, "She hasn't woken up yet."

The weight of her words pressed down on me like an avalanche, leaving me speechless and overwhelmed by a gut-wrenching sense of dread.

Cookie and I walked upstairs and she led me down the hallway outside Elena's room. There, a man sat on a chair. When he noticed Cookie, he jumped up, rushing to offer her some coffee. She accepted it hesitantly before turning to me.

"This is Tony. He's a friend of Elena and me," she said. "Tony, this is Manny."

The man offered a sad smile as he shook me.

"Elena's parents left Baileys Harbor years ago, but her father and mother will be arriving tomorrow. I called them," Cookie said before she took a sip of the coffee.

I glanced around, still trying to process the overwhelming fear gnawing at my insides. That meant, until then, all Elena had was Cookie, Tony and me.

"Do you want some coffee?" Tony asked but I shook my head and looked up at the door. All I wanted was to see Elena's smile.

Just then, a doctor walked out of the room and the three of us converged around him.

"I'm afraid Miss Foster sustained some significant injuries in the accident," he said, looking down at his notes. "She suffered a severe impact to the back of her head, resulting in head trauma. The initial scans show no signs of internal bleeding, but we'll need to monitor her closely."

"Head trauma? What does that mean exactly?" Tony asked in a concerned tone.

"Well, head trauma can lead to various complications, such as concussions, swelling, and potential neurological issues. We've conducted a thorough examination, including a CT scan, to assess any immediate risks."

The words hung heavily in the air, and my mind struggled to comprehend the extent of the situation. I could barely hear the doctor's voice, let alone formulate a response.

"Is she going to be, okay?" Cookie asked.

The doctor paused briefly before he spoke. "We're doing all we can, but I must be honest; it's a critical situation." He glanced at me. "We've stabilized her for now, but Elena has not regained consciousness. At this point, all we can do is wait for her to wake up. We'll be monitoring her closely, but it's important to prepare for a lengthy recovery process."

"Oh God, oh God," Cookie muttered as she moved to sit on the chair. Tony walked over to her and tried to comfort her. While I stood in front of the doctor, my heart pounding louder than ever before.

Elena wasn't waking up.

Elena had to wake up.

"Can we see her?" I heard Cookie ask and the doctor agreed. Then she turned to me. "Manny, you should go see her. I need to call for security before the press finds out about this."

I nodded subconsciously. Then I entered Elena's room with a heavy heart, my breath catching at the sight of her lying on the bed, so fragile and still. She lay on the hospital bed, her body frail and battered. Her head was encased in a protective brace, and a bandage covered a significant injury on the back of her head. Bruises marked her face, and her right arm was immobilized in a sling. Tubes and wires snaked from her body to various machines, monitoring her injuries and vital signs.

My heart broke.

I walked up to her, taking her hand gently in mine, and my fingers trembled as I looked down at her face.

"Come on, Star," I whispered, my voice shaky. "You have to wake up. You're strong, and you can't just come into my life and leave like this. I won't let you." I sounded desperate but I didn't care.

I placed my forehead on the edge of the bed. "Please, Elena, wake up," I repeated over and over. "I'll do anything, just please, wake up."

As I continued to beg, I felt a slight movement in her hand. My heart leaped with hope, and I moved quickly to her side. Her eyelids fluttered, and then her eyes flickered open. "Elena!" I called out, relief flooding my voice. "Baby, you're awake."

I didn't waste a second and called for Cookie, urgently telling her that Elena had woken up and to get the doctor immediately. Then I turned back to my star. She moaned softly. "S...so loud," She mumbled.

I chuckled. "I'm sorry," I said, my voice filled with overwhelming relief. I pressed a gentle kiss to her hand. "I'm so sorry."

Elena opened her eyes. Then she blinked and blinked, trying to focus. Her gaze finally landed on me, but her brows furrowed in confusion.

I sighed in relief. "Star," I said.

She glanced at her hands in mine and her voice was shaky when she asked, "Who are you?"

CHAPTER FIFTEEN
ELENA

I woke up in a sterile room, my vision blurred as I tried to make sense of my surroundings. Panic bubbled within me as I realized I didn't know where I was or how I got here. More importantly, I didn't know the man standing beside me.

His grip on my hand was tight and desperate. His eyes, deep and filled with an anguish I couldn't comprehend, bore into mine. He looked at me as if something inside him had shattered into a million pieces. And he was undeniably handsome. I scolded myself for even thinking that.

He looked like a kid.

Desperation laced his voice as he stammered, "W-what?"

I glanced at our hands again and frowned. "Who are you?" I asked. "W-what am I doing h-here?"

He let go off my hand quickly, like it was hot to touch. Then he took two steps back and quivered. For a moment, he seemed at a loss for words. Then, with a voice full of tenderness and love, he softly called, "Elena."

He knew my name. The warmth in his voice sent a comforting shiver down my spine, though I couldn't fathom why.

Before I could ask how he knew me, the door swung open, and a familiar face entered the room. Relief washed over me as I recognized her.

"Cookie," I smiled.

Cookie rushed over, enveloping me in a comforting hug. It was a sense of normalcy in this situation.

"Are you okay?" She asked.

"I guess," I said, smiling.

Beside Cookie, a doctor appeared. "Good day, Miss Foster, I'm Doctor Woods. Can you tell me how you're feeling right now? Any pain or discomfort?" He asked in a kind tone.

I shook my head. "Uh, no... I don't think so. I mean, nothing major."

Dr. Woods smiled. "That's good to hear," he said before scribbling something in his notepad. "Do you have any headaches or dizziness?"

I hesitated before responding. "Well, maybe a slight headache, but it's not too bad."

He nodded, "Alright, thank you for letting me know. Can you recall what happened before you woke up here?"

I frowned. That was odd. I didn't remember much. "It's all a bit hazy," I said.

The gap in my memory left me feeling disoriented.

"It's not uncommon to experience memory gaps after an accident. We'll work on that," Dr. Woods said, "Now, do you recognize the people who were with you when you woke up?"

Curiosity gnawed at me, and I couldn't help but steal a glance at the man who had been clutching my hand with such desperation earlier.

His gaze locked onto mine, a strange and intense look in his eyes that I couldn't quite decipher. Unsettled, I looked away.

"Sort of. I know Cookie, she's, my friend. But him..." I answered.

"She doesn't remember me," The stranger said in a strained voice.

I blinked. Was I supposed to?

Dr. Woods' frown deepened as he turned his scrutiny toward me.

He threw me a seemingly simple question: "What's today's date?"

I furrowed my brows, trying to recall. After a moment's pause, I tentatively replied, "It's the 6th of January, 2022."

Cookie gasped softly, and the doctor's eyes widened. It was as if my answer had triggered something significant, though I couldn't understand why.

"What's wrong?" I asked. "Is something wrong with me?"

Dr. Woods wrote in his notepad and then he said, "Please leave the room. I need to ask Miss Foster a couple of questions."

Cookie's gaze was filled with worry as she motioned to walk out. I clutched her hand tightly. "I'm scared," I admitted with a quiver in my voice.

She turned to me smiled, but it was a sad and empathetic smile. "You'll be fine, Elena. Just listen to the doctor."

I nodded, wanting to believe her words. But something nagged at me. I didn't remember how I got here and from their reactions, that wasn't the only thing I didn't remember. What if I had forgotten important stuff?

Desperation prompted my next question, "Where's Caleb?"

Cookie's eyes widened, and my heart ached as my eyes welled up with tears. The mere mention of his name triggered an intense emotional response within me. I wasn't sure why. Did I need him?

What was going on?

She glanced at the doctor and the stranger in the room before tucking a loose strand of my hair behind my ear. "He should be on his way, Elena. Don't worry," She reassured me.

The thought of Caleb's arrival provided a measure of comfort. He was my boyfriend. Things would start to make sense if I saw him, or so I hoped.

As Cookie left the room with the stranger, I couldn't resist casting one more glance in his direction. His eyes bore into mine, an unsettling mix of anger, hurt, and something else I couldn't quite place. It unnerved me, made my heart race. I wanted to ask him why he was looking at me that way, why it stirred such complicated emotions within me.

Before I could muster the courage to speak, the man clenched his jaw and stormed out of the room. Left alone with the doctor, I clung to the hope that he would tell me what was happening.

***

I never saw the stranger again, but that fact hardly occupied my thoughts. The doctor's revelation had shaken me to my core—I had lost eight months of memories, and that was an unsettling chasm in my life that I couldn't ignore.

Eight months, an entire chapter of my life, erased. I didn't know what to make of this newfound void. It felt like losing something significant, something essential, but I couldn't even remember what that something was.

A single tear trickled down my cheek, and I instinctively wiped it away with the small cloth that rested nearby. At that moment, a gentle touch grazed my shoulder, and I turned to see my mom.

With eyes that mirrored my own, her green gaze bore into mine. She said, "You're crying again, mija"

I sniffled. "I don't even know why," I confessed.

Her response was kind and reassuring. "It's okay. Sometimes, you just need to let it out."

My mother's presence in the hospital room was a comfort that transcended words. It was often said that I was a spitting image of her, and when I looked at her now, I couldn't deny the resemblance. Her ebony hair was neatly tied in a bun, the white streaks gracefully accentuating the black strands. Deep green eyes peered at me from a face adorned with slight wrinkles.

She reached for the small saucer on the bedside table and presented me with apple slices, just as she had when I was a child. I smiled. At least I remembered that.

"Thank you," I muttered as I accepted the apple slices and began to eat.

Suddenly, the hospital room door swung open, and a small entourage entered. Alongside my father, there was Cookie. And then there was Caleb.

"We're back!" He sang and I smiled.

My father's tender gaze met my mother's, and he leaned in to plant a gentle kiss on her forehead. Their love had always been something I admired and longed for—a bond that had drawn me to Baileys Harbor, where they had first met.

Cookie had mentioned that she and I had been living in a house here for the past six months. I had no doubt it was a decision I made. I always wanted to live in the town my parents met. But a pang of sadness hit me because I couldn't remember any of it. It was as though a part of my life had been stolen, and I didn't even know what I had lost.

Caleb's fingers sifted gently through my hair, and for a moment, I welcomed the familiarity of his touch. But as I looked up at him, my smile faltered. Something felt off, out of place, though I couldn't quite pinpoint it. The usually warm and comforting sensation that enveloped me in his presence had been replaced by a disconcerting feeling.

"You okay?" He asked.

Ever since Caleb had appeared at the hospital two days ago, a sense of unease had settled deep within me. It clung to my chest like a shadow, casting doubt on everything around me. It was as though my instincts were trying to warn me of something, something elusive.

I looked away from him. "I'm fine," I said.

"The doctor said you won't have to spend a lot of time here," he said. "I think you deserve a break."

"A break?" I asked.

He nodded. "I propose a trip to the Whispering Pines. You may not remember it but it's a place you love. We've gone together a couple of times. You bought a cabin there a couple of months ago."

I blinked. I didn't remember that. The idea sounded appealing, and yet, it stirred something within me, something I couldn't quite grasp.

"Is this cabin safe?" My mother asked.

"It's in the woods. Elena loved going there so I think it'll be good for her."

My mind drew a blank when I thought of Whispering Pines. Yet, there was something about the cabin, that gnawed at me. It was an insistent and unsettling sensation.

Glancing around the room, I noticed Cookie's gaze fixed on Caleb, her eyes filled with a mixture of resentment and mistrust. I frowned at that. Something really was wrong. Cookie had been acting weird towards Caleb ever since he arrived and they talked to the doctor. Even my father, once warm and welcoming, now appeared distant.

Cookie suddenly smiled and it took me by surprise. "You know, you're right Caleb," she said. "I think Elena should go to Whispering Pines. It would be good for her," She added in a voice that sent shivers down my spine.

Her support for the idea contradicted the unease I felt, and I couldn't help but wonder if she knew something I didn't.

Caleb's reaction mirrored my confusion, his grimace and frown directed at Cookie. "Uh...yeah," He nodded.

I couldn't be certain if my parents sensed the tension in the room, but I certainly did.

Cookie's phone suddenly rang and she excused herself to answer a phone call. My mind returned to the cabin once more. I didn't even remember what it looked like but it felt like there was something bigger that I wasn't remembering.

I turned to Caleb. "Maybe we should go to Whispering Pines," I said.

He smiled and nodded in agreement, planting a kiss on my forehead. But as his lips touched my skin, an unexpected discomfort welled up inside me, a sensation I couldn't quite place.

He smiled at me. "Don't worry. I'll be with you, and we'll have the best time together," he said.

His words didn't evoke the warmth I had anticipated. Instead, they left me feeling uneasy, trapped in a web of confusion that seemed to have no end.

C HAPTER SIXTEEN
MANNY

Elena didn't remember me.

Sitting in the sterile reception of the hospital, I felt like a stranger in a world that had suddenly turned cold and unfamiliar. Everything around me was a blur of white walls, hushed voices, and the antiseptic scent that seemed to permeate the air.

I had been lost for a few days now. The woman I had grown to care for, the woman who had ignited a fire within my heart, now saw me as nothing more than a stranger. I wasn't sure if there was any pain greater than knowing that the person you wanted could no longer recognize you.

"Manny."

I looked up to see Cookie and rose from my seat quickly. Her eyes softened when they met mine, and I noticed they were tainted with pity.

Pity for me.

Swallowing the lump in my throat, I struggled to find my voice. "How is she?" I asked, trying to sound strong and composed.

"She's still awake and thankfully, she's doing well," she said.

"And..."

"She still can't remember the past few months."

Her words sent a shiver down my spine. I let out a weary sigh, my shoulders slumping in resignation. The doctor had already explained that Elena's memories needed to return naturally and though it may take time, she had to remember everything on her own.

I had never felt even more helpless in my life.

"We're just going to have to wait and hope," Cookie said as we sat next to each other. "The doctor says Elena's mental state is fragile and delicate. Pushing too hard could confuse her."

That was the reason why I stayed away, why I didn't visit her even when all I wanted to do was hold and kiss her. I wanted to remind her of everything I felt for her and all the things she said she felt for me. But to Elena, Caleb was her boyfriend.

"I hate that Caleb is here," Cookie said as if she could read my mind.

A pang of anger and jealousy welled up within me. Caleb had shown up at the hospital when he heard about Elena's accident and he was exploiting the situation, pretending to be the perfect boyfriend. It infuriated me.

"Is he with her right now?" I asked.

"Yeah," Cookie said. "And it's annoying seeing him dote on her like he didn't hurt her. Elena was in the process of firing and suing him just before the accident."

I glanced at Cookie. "What?"

She nodded. "It's a whole lot but now she doesn't even remember that. He's trying to slip into her life."

While I remained a forgotten stranger.

My chest hurt and I ran a hand through my hair. "Fuck, I want to see her," I said.

"Manny..."

"I need to see her," I said, my voice breaking.

She was silent for a while before she said, "Maybe you can see her. You can introduce yourself as a friend of hers. It may not be enough but..."

"It won't confuse her," I said. "Yeah, that might be a good idea," I added, even though I hated the idea. "I'll just introduce myself as a friend. She doesn't have to know what we were."

"Do you want to go now?" She asked.

I shook my head. I wasn't sure I could stay in that room with Elena and Caleb without feeling like I wanted to punch him in the face.

Cookie's eyes held sympathy as she nodded in agreement. "Take your time, Manny. This is hard for all of us, but we'll do everything we can to protect Elena right now."

"Thank you, Cookie," I murmured.

As she left the hospital's lobby, I sank back into my thoughts, grappling with the heartache that threatened to consume me. I considered going after her, following her up to Elena's room but seeing Elena with Caleb, acting as though he was the love of her life, was a torment I wasn't sure I could bear.

My phone rang and I sighed. I knew immediately that it was Omar and I was late for my shift. I stood and left the hospital. As I drove to the fire station, I couldn't help but wonder what I would do if Elena never remembered me.

When I arrived at the fire station, a sense of guilt washed over me. Alarms were blaring, and firefighters were rushing out, gearing up for an emergency. I waited for the rush of adrenaline that coursed through my veins in times like this but there was nothing.

I saw Omar as I got out of the car and hurried over to him. "Omar, I'm really sorry for being late," I began. "I-"

He glared at me. "Manny, we have an emergency right now," he snapped. "We'll talk about this later."

I clenched my jaw as he walked past me. Then went into the fire station. I found a bench and slumped onto it, feeling utterly helpless.

Kelly's face appeared above me. "Aren't you going out with them?" she asked.

I shook my head. "No, not this time," I replied quietly.

"Are you okay?" She tilted her head and asked.

No.

"Yeah," I said.

I waited impatiently on that bench, my thoughts a jumble of worry. It wasn't long before Omar and the rest of the guys returned. They all looked tired.

"Manny," Omar called, "Captain's office."

His face bore a frown I didn't like as I followed him. When we got to the office, he began to remove his gear, his weariness evident in his every movement. I observed him silently, a pang of guilt gnawing at me. Omar was doing a great job as acting captain and I was slacking.

"I'm sorry," I muttered.

He glanced at me. "Sit down, Manny," he instructed.

As I sat, the door swung open, revealing Liam, another one of our fellow firefighters. "Omar, we have dinner plans," he said without looking up from his phone. "Marge says to remind you not to forget the shrimp." He looked up from his phone and his brows creased when he saw me. "Hey Manny," he said, tilting his head. "What are you doing here?"

I ignored his question. "You two have dinner plans?" I grinned.

Liam was married to Omar's sister, Marge who just so happened to be best friends with Omar's wife, Jenn. Liam and Omar didn't get along before but lately you could always find them together and I had a feeling they were now closer than they would like to admit.

"Weekly dinner with Marge and Jenn," Liam answered. "Jenn gets scary when we're late."

Omar sighed as checked the time on his phone. "We don't have much time," He said before turned to me, his expression a mix of concern and frustration, and finally asked the question that had been looming over me since I walked into the station: "Manny, what the hell is going on?"

I remained silent as Liam settled into chair next to me, "Why are you asking him that? Did something happen?"

I sighed, "I'll fix it."

Omar's voice was stern as he responded, "You better."

He then took a seat behind the captain's desk and took a deep breath. He ran his fingers through his hair. "Manny, if you need help or want to talk about anything, you know you can."

Great. Now, I was the guy who needed help.

I stared at him for a moment, gathering my thoughts. Finally, I asked, "What would you do if Jenn woke up tomorrow morning and didn't remember who you were?"

Liam chimed in, humorously, "He'd kill everybody."

Despite the heaviness in my heart, I couldn't help but chuckle at that. Omar shot him a glare, and I waited for his answer.

Omar's eyes softened, like it always did when his wife was mentioned and he said, "I'd remind her."

I swallowed hard. "What if she doesn't remember?"

He shrugged. "I won't think about that. I'd just keep reminding her. I love her, Manny. If you love someone, you don't give up on them. Scratch that, you can't. You do everything you can to help them remember."

Love was such a crazy thing to consider. I wasn't even sure I was there yet with Elena, but I needed her to remember me. The fact that she didn't make me feel so small and invisible.

Manny Delgado was never small or invisible.

I offered Omar a weak smile. "I'm sorry I haven't been at my best lately. I'll do better."

He nodded, his expression softening. "It's okay."

"You two enjoy your dinner," I said to him and Laim.

As I walked out of the captain's office, my phone chimed with a new message. I checked it, and my heart lifted at the sight of a picture from Cookie. It was Elena, sitting and eating. The following message read: "She's eating better, and the doctor says she's healing fast. She might get released soon!"

A smile spread across my face as I stared at the picture. I couldn't help but rub my thumb gently over her face on the screen, whispering to her, "See you soon, Star."

***

I stood in front of Elena's house, taking a deep breath before I raised my hand to knock on the door. The anticipation was building up inside me, and my heart raced. When the door swung open, Cookie greeted me with a warm smile. "Hey Manny," She said, "Come on in."

I walked in and from inside the house, I heard Elena's voice, "Cookie, who is that?"

My pulse quickened, and I couldn't help but feel a rush of nervousness and excitement all at once.

As she came into view, my heart did a somersault. She looked fresh out of the shower, her hair tied up, and she was wearing a cozy sweatshirt paired with shorts. I couldn't tear my gaze away from her.

Elena's eyes widened as she saw me, and for a moment, there seemed to be a glimmer of recognition in her beautiful eyes. She said softly, "It's you."

Hope surged within me, and I asked, "Me?"

She nodded, her expression thoughtful. "Yeah, you were at the hospital," she said.

My heart sank a bit. She didn't really remember me, but I maintained a friendly smile. "Yeah, I was," I said, "I'm Manuel Delgado and I'm sorry for leaving back then but I really couldn't believe you didn't remember me."

Elena looked at me and with a warm smile, she said, "Manuel."

I couldn't help but smile back, and my heart fluttered when she used my full name. It felt so formal though. I extended my hand towards her. "You can call me Manny," I said, my voice gentle.

Her hand slipped into mine, and she repeated, "Manny."

Hearing her say my name again sent a pleasant shiver down my spine. I missed the sound of it.

From behind us, Cookie chimed in. "Manny is our friend. You don't remember him but he's a firefighter and some time ago, he saved you, Elena. You guys started hanging out after that."

Elena's gaze shifted back to me, "Really? That's amazing," she said, her eyes widening in surprise. "Thank you. I'm sorry I've been acting weird," she said.

"It's alright," I assured her. "I completely understand."

"I invited him over for dinner," Cookie announced. Then she glanced at me. "Did you bring the wine?" She asked.

I raised the paper bag with the bottle in my hand. "I found the one you asked for," I said. Cookie took it eagerly. "I'll go put it in ice," she said.

As she headed into the kitchen, leaving Elena and me alone in the living room, I couldn't help but steal a quick glance at Elena. Despite the initial awkwardness, I was eager to spend more time with her. We stood there for a moment, just staring at each other. There was a peculiar mixture of familiarity and uncertainty in the air. After a brief pause, she broke the silence.

"Would you like to go to the living room?" she asked, her voice soft.

I nodded and followed her as she led the way. "Are you feeling better?" I asked.

She replied with a nod. "Yeah, but I still have to go for checkups, which are very annoying," she said, her tone carrying a hint of frustration. "But it's fine since my parents are around."

I was glad she didn't mention Caleb. "Where are your parents?" I asked.

"They're out tonight," she said.

As we entered the living room, Elena accidentally bumped into the side of a nearby stool, and I reacted quickly, catching her before she could fall. Time seemed to stand still for a moment as our eyes locked. I could see a softness in her gaze, a vulnerability that tugged at my heart.

It was nostalgic.

"Be careful," I murmured. Then I smiled at a memory. "You're still as clumsy as ever," I said.

Elena continued to stare into my eyes, and I couldn't help but feel drawn to her. I wanted to close the distance between our lips, to hug her and tell her I missed her, even though she was here.

"Are you okay?" I asked softly, even though what I actually wanted to say was different.

She stared at me for a moment and she nodded, her voice barely above a whisper as she said, "Thank you, Manny."

CHAPTER SEVENTEEN

ELENA

Watching Manny and Cookie laugh together as they headed towards the door, I couldn't help but feel a pang in my chest. That sensation had been lingering ever since he arrived, and it was both confusing and disconcerting. Cookie had said Manny was a friend of ours, but I couldn't help but feel like there was something else. I saw it in the way he looked at me.

Manny paused and turned around, his gaze softening as our eyes met.

There it was.

I blinked, momentarily lost in his deep, expressive eyes. He was undeniably handsome and had a youthful charm about him. Cookie said we were friends, and I initially doubted it, thinking we had nothing in common. Yet, Manny was surprisingly easy to get along with, and he had a sense of humor that could make me laugh effortlessly. It was more than Caleb had done since I got back home.

"I should go clean up," Cookie said, "Can you escort Manny out, Elena?"

I nodded and she left us alone again. The atmosphere grew awkward, just as it had the first time we were left alone. I glanced at him, curiosity gnawing at me.

As we walked out of the house, I asked, "What's it like being a fireman? Isn't it dangerous?"

His gaze was fixed on his car as he answered, "Yeah, it can be. But, you know, I like the danger."

I arched an eyebrow. "You like it? How could you possibly like something so risky?"

A sly smile tugged at the corners of Manny's lips as he replied, "I guess I have a thing for going after things that could hurt me. Jobs, women..." His words hung in the air, and his gaze bore into mine for a moment too long.

I felt a blush creeping onto my cheeks, my heart fluttering in response to his intense gaze.

Focus Elena.

"Are you really doing okay, Elena?" he asked, his voice gentle.

I nodded shyly, my voice barely a whisper. "Yes, I am."

Manny smiled. "That's good. That's all that matters," he said softly. He reached out to tuck a loose strand of hair behind my ear before saying, "Go inside. You'll catch a cold."

Those words struck a chord in my mind. A vivid memory resurfaced: me standing outside a cabin in a forest, Manny telling me those exact words. The rush of memories and emotions was overwhelming, but I couldn't quite grasp them.

"Elena?" He called my name, snapping me out of my daze. "What happened?"

I blinked at him and replied, "Nothing."

He was at the cabin? Was it the same one Caleb wanted us to visit?

Manny nodded. "Alright then. Goodnight, Elena."

"Goodnight."

As I watched him walk away, there was a pang in my chest. But now I knew something that could help me trigger my memories.

I needed to visit the cabin.

***

As I approached Caleb's downtown office, a sense of unease washed over me. The sleek, modern office building seemed somewhat out of place in our quaint town of Baileys Harbor. Caleb had told me while I was still at the hospital that he had moved to the town for me and he thought we should go back to New York. I realized now what kind of sacrifice he had made. Caleb's polished image didn't quite match the easygoing vibe of the Baileys Harbor.

I entered the building and found myself in a spacious lobby with marble floors. The reception desk was sleek and minimalist, and a friendly receptionist greeted me with a warm smile. I thanked her and made my way to the elevator.

Caleb's office was on the fifth floor, and as I rode the elevator up, my thoughts swirled with questions about him and us. He had been distant lately, and his recent lack of communication had left me feeling uncertain and incomplete. Last night when I told him we needed to talk, I was surprised he even responded.

When I reached the fifth floor, I stepped out into a well-lit hallway with plush carpeting. His office door was adorned with a polished bronze plaque bearing his name: Caleb Norman, Artist Manager.

My heart pounded in my chest as I approached the door to Caleb's office. I was about to knock when I heard them—the unmistakable sounds of sex coming from within. Gasping, I quickly stepped away from the door, my heart racing in disbelief.

"Oh fuck," The woman gasped.

The sounds were clear and vivid, leaving no room for doubt. Her moans mingled with Caleb's grunts, and it was so intimate, yet they felt distant, almost surreal, as if I were eavesdropping on a scene from someone else's life.

Not my boyfriend's.

"Cum inside me please," The woman whimpered.

I was frozen in place, my ears tuned into every sigh and whisper, unable to tear myself away from the painful truth unfolding before me. When they finally finished, I still couldn't move.

"You should leave now," Caleb's voice was stern. "Elena will be here soon."

"Are you serious?" The woman asked, "I thought she left you. I heard she was in an accident a while ago. Is that true?"

His reply was matter-of-fact. "Yeah. And thanks to that, she doesn't know that she left me right now. She doesn't remember anything."

There was a brief pause before she asked, "She doesn't remember that she caught you cheating? Or that she was going to fire and sue you?"

What?

I struggled to breathe, my mind reeling from the shock of what I had just heard. My memory remained frustratingly blank, offering no context or explanation for what I was hearing and I hated it.

Tears welled up in my eyes as I backed away from the door. I needed answers, but I had no idea where to find them or how to piece them.

"I know that bitch, Cookie is only holding back right now because she doesn't want to confuse Elena but it won't be long before she starts sending lawyers over here again to bother me," Caleb said.

My heart pounded loudly in my chest. Cookie knew?

"I hate that bitch," He added.

"What's your plan?" the woman asked with a teasing tone.

Caleb's response was chilling in its candor. "For now, I'm gathering as much money as I can from Elena's profits, and then I'll leave."

Her laughter rang in the air. "You taking me with you baby?" She asked playfully.

He chuckled, "Anywhere you want."

The fucking asshole. I gritted my teeth as I burst into the room, my entire body quivering with rage. The woman shrieked in surprise, hurriedly hiding her nakedness behind the desk.

"You asshole!" I shouted, my voice shaking with emotion.

Caleb's face registered shock, his mouth agape as he said, "E-Elena?" He glanced around. "Why are you so early?"

I glanced at the woman behind the desk. She was young, pretty and I couldn't believe it but it made me feel so fucking small and insecure.

"You're disgusting! You're evil!" I yelled, my voice filled with a mixture of hurt and anger. "And you're going to pay!"

"Elena, calm down. I can explain," Caleb said but I wasn't going to listen. I couldn't believe I had been so blind, so trusting.

So, fucking stupid.

The world felt like a whirlwind as I rushed out of Caleb's office, my heart pounding, and tears stinging my eyes. I had to get out of there.

Caleb's voice called out to me from behind, "Elena, wait," He pleaded. But waiting was the last thing I wanted to do.

As I approached the elevator, I realized it was still on its way up. Waiting for it would give Caleb a chance to catch up to me, and I didn't want that. My instincts took over, and I veered toward the stairs, determined to put as much distance between us as possible.

Before I could reach the top of the stairs, Caleb's hand wrapped around my arm, his fingers closing in a vice-like grip. "I said fucking wait!" He sneered. "You have to listen to me," He added.

Fury boiled within me. "Let me go!" I yelled at him, my voice quivering with anger and hurt.

His grip tightened. "You need to calm down. You're being hysterical," he said insisted. "Other people in the building might hear us."

I didn't care. I wanted them to know what a despicable person he was. "They should hear!" I cried out, my voice trembling with emotion. "Let them know what you've done, taking advantage of the fact that I didn't remember anything."

Caleb's eyes darkened. "I had no choice! I was only trying to help you, even after you kicked me to the curb, even after you kissed that stupid fireman!"

Manny?

My vision blurred with tears as the full weight of his betrayal settled over me. My voice quivered as I said, "I can't believe you did this to me, after everything we've been through together."

Caleb just stared at me, a blank expression on his face, but his jaw was clenched. He asked in a cold tone, "So, what now? Do you want me to let you go?"

Tears streamed down my cheeks as I said, "Yes, let me go."

He chuckled and shook his head. "You know what Elena? You never should have survived."

"W-What?" I asked.

Caleb's grip on my arm suddenly released and I was sent tumbling backward down the stairs. The world spun around me in a chaotic blur, and a terrified scream tore from my throat, echoing through the stairwell. I tried to grab onto the railing, but my hands grasped at thin air.

My heart pounded relentlessly, matching the frenetic pace of my descent. The cold, unforgiving steps seemed to stretch out endlessly before me. It was a nightmarish freefall, each jarring collision between my body and the unforgiving stairs met with sharp, searing pain.

Then, in an instant, it was over.

I crashed violently into a glass statue at the base of the stairs, shattering it into countless shards. The world around me seemed to come alive with voices, distant yet urgent.

"What happened?"

"Who is that?"

The sensation of warm liquid trickling down my head sent a shiver of dread down my spine. *Blood.* Pain radiated from various points on my body and my entire being ached with an intensity that was almost unbearable.

As consciousness slipped away, my thoughts fragmented. Amid the chaos and agony, one memory surfaced, so hauntingly vivid that I knew it was not mistake: Manny's face, right before his lips collided with mine.

CHAPTER EIGHTEEN
ELENA

As my eyelids fluttered open, I was greeted by the sight of Manny's warm and comforting gaze. His lips curved into a beautiful smile. "Hey star, you're awake," he said softly.

A soft grin tugged at my lips as I sleepily replied, "What time is it?" Manny glanced at the nearby clock. "It's 3 pm."

I sat up abruptly. "Why didn't you wake me up earlier?" I chided him. "I need to be at the studio in half an hour."

His smile deepened, and he leaned closer. "Because I was enjoying watching you sleep."

Heat crept into my cheeks, and I playfully rolled my eyes. "You're ridiculous," I teased, feigning annoyance. I had spent the day until that point with him.

Manny reached out and pulled me gently toward him, planting a soft kiss on my forehead. His warm breath on my skin sent shivers down my spine. "Five more minutes?" he requested, his voice low and persuasive.

I hesitated for a moment, feeling his arms around me, but then I reluctantly pulled away. "No," I replied, trying to sound firm.

He sighed dramatically, feigning disappointment. "One day," he said, "you'll be so whipped for me that you'll skip work just to be with me."

I chuckled at his playful arrogance. "And how do you plan on doing that?" I teased as I got off the bed.

Manny's eyes sparkled mischievously. "Easy," he said, turning his attention to his phone. "I'll be so good to you that you'll fall in love with me."

I blinked, taken aback by his words, but he didn't seem to notice as he was already engrossed in his phone. My heart raced but I ignored it as I walked over to the bathroom.

Love.

Did he really want me to fall in love with him?

My eyes flickered open, and I found myself in a familiar yet disorienting room. The sterile white walls of the hospital surrounded me, and the faint beeping of machines told me where I was. Blinking away the grogginess, I realized there were tears in my eyes.

I had been crying because I missed Manny, even when my conscious mind didn't remember him. My memories of him were still a bit jumbled. It was as if my heart recognized something that my mind was still trying to piece together, and it was letting it all out.

As the door creaked open, my heart skipped a beat. Cookie walked in first. Behind her were my parents and when they saw me, their eyes widened.

My mother's voice quivered with emotion as she rushed to my bedside. "I'm so glad you're awake, Mija," she said, her eyes welling up with tears. "Are you okay? How are you feeling?"

I couldn't help but smile. "I'm fine mommy," I said. My body hurt a bit but it was definitely better than when I woke up after the accident. "I really need to stop ending up in the hospital," I added.

Cookie crossed her arms and chimed in. "Touche, Elena. You do keep giving us all heart attacks."

I smiled at her and she smiled back, though her eyes were filled with worry.

My father simply pulled me into a heartfelt embrace. He didn't say anything for a while and I didn't think I needed him to. "The doctor will be here soon. We were just talking to him, are you hurt?" He said as he released me.

Feeling a bit more composed, I said, "There's a little pain but not really. Did the doctor say it was bad? My injuries, I mean."

My mother's voice quivered as she replied, "Thankfully, you didn't break anything this time, but you did hit your head again."

My father's eyes bore into mine with a mix of worry and relief. "I hope nothing bad happened again," he muttered, concern etched in his features.

I shook my head and offered a small smile. "No, Dad, quite the opposite, actually. I remember a few things now, like the first time I caught Caleb cheating."

Turning to Cookie, I saw a furrow in her brow. "Caleb ran away before the police got to his office. Some people say they saw him push you."

My mother's eyes widened in shock as she asked, "Is that true?" Her voice trembled with anger.

My own emotions were a whirlwind, and I replied, "I don't want to dwell on it right now. He did let me go so I could fall. I don't remember everything yet."

My father grumbled under his breath. "That asshole. I'm going to kill him."

I turned my attention back to Cookie. "I want to know about the lawsuit between me and Caleb. Please, Cookie, tell me everything, and don't hold anything back. I'm ready to face it all now."

She closed her eyes, tapped her afro with both eyes gently and took a deep breath. "Thank God you remember a bit now because I was tired of holding back from that bastard."

Exhaustion crept over me as my family and Cookie continued their discussions about Caleb and the lawsuit. They finally decided to let me rest. God knows I needed it. My eyelids grew heavy, and I welcomed the opportunity to escape into sleep.

However, when I opened my eyes again, I knew immediately that there was a presence in the room, a presence I felt more than saw. The familiar scent filled my senses, and I knew instantly who it was. Manny.

My gaze moved to him. And his eyes flickered with rage. "Manny," I called.

He didn't respond. He just stared at me.

"What are you doing?" I asked and he replied, "I don't know. I'm trying to be your friend."

I couldn't help but shake my head. "You're not my friend," I told him, my voice wavering with emotions I couldn't quite understand. "Don't ever call yourself that again."

Manny watched me carefully, his gaze penetrating. "You remember me," he said and it was more a statement than a question.

I nodded hesitantly. "A bit," I admitted.

He took a step closer, closing some of the distance between us. "How much?" He asked.

"I don't remember how we met but I know we spent time at the cabin together and we were together after," I said, remembering the time I spent in his house.

Manny's eyes sparkled with a mix of hope and desire, and he asked, "So, you remember my kisses then?"

My heart raced as I hesitated for a moment, and then I nodded. In that instant, Manny leaned in and kissed me deeply, igniting a fire within me as I rediscovered the attraction that had drawn me to him in the first place.

His lips were warm and soft against mine, and his mouth moved with a gentle urgency that sent shivers down my spine. His fingers tangled in my hair, pulling me closer, and I responded with equal fervor, wrapping my arms around his neck. Our tongues danced together, a silent conversation of desire and need. The taste of him, the feel of his body pressed against mine, it all felt so right.

My heart raced as he released me. "It took you long enough, Star," he said with a playful smile.

I took a shaky breath, still trying to process the whirlwind of emotions that had just washed over me. "I can't believe I forgot you," I confessed, my voice filled with regret. I couldn't believe I forgot how it felt to be around him.

Manny's expression softened even further, and he placed a gentle finger under my chin, tilting my face up to meet his gaze. "Hey, there's no need to apologize," he said softly. "I'm just glad you remember me now."

His words were soothing but I wanted to make things right, to erase the pain that had marred our time apart.

"I missed you so much," He continued, his eyes locked onto mine. "You have no idea how much it hurt to see you with that bastard."

"Caleb..."

"I heard about what he did from Cookie," Manny said, clenching his jaw.

My heart pounded. "Let's not talk about that right now," I said.

I just wanted to be with him.

He nodded without hesitation and a radiant smile spreading across his face. "You have no idea how much I missed you," he said.

Tears welled up in my eyes again, but this time they were tears of gratitude and relief. "How can I make it up to you?" I asked.

Manny wiped my tears away with his thumb, his gaze flickering to my lips for a moment. "When you get out of here," He said, "You can say yes when I ask you to be my girlfriend."

I tilted my head. "Really?"

He smirked playfully but didn't respond. Instead, he pulled me into a warm embrace. Our bodies pressed close, fitting together as if they were always meant to be this way. And for the first time since I woke up after the first accident, I felt safe, cherished, and complete.

C HAPTER NINETEEN
MANNY

I dashed through the hotel lobby, bypassing the elevator for the stairs. I was still in the clothes I had worn to work which wasn't part of the plan. But Omar had me working tirelessly as punishment for slacking off. I couldn't even leave the station a minute before my shift ended.

I hoped Elena wasn't ready yet, though. She had a show that was set to start soon, and I wanted to see her before she got on stage. Actually, I promised I would. It was her first public appearance since she lost her memories and I wanted to be there.

I headed to the fourth floor and my forehead tricked with sweat by the time I got there. Then I found the room she said she would be in. I knocked once before the door swung open, revealing her father standing there, his gaze locked onto me. Despite the polite smile on my face, I could feel the weight of his scrutiny. We had met briefly at the hospital when Elena had first woken up after her first accident.

Cookie introduced us but I was still reeling in from the fact that she had forgotten me to even try to connect with her parents.

"Good evening, Mr. Foster," I greeted him, my tone warm and respectful. He continued to study me, unblinking, his expression giving nothing away.

We continued to maintain eye contact for a while and truth be told, my eyes were beginning to water at the sides. Was he a staring contest champion? Was this his way of asserting dominance?

"Manuel," he said in an accent I didn't quite recognize. "You're late."

I rubbed the back of my head nervously. "Yeah, I know. But I had work and well..."

Another figure stepped up next to him and I smiled. Elena's mother was gentler than her husband was not to mention kinder.

"Oh, hello Manny," She beamed. "You're here."

"Good evening, ma'am," I said to her, my voice softening as I added, "You look beautiful as ever."

Her blush only deepened as she thanked me, and I couldn't help but smile warmly at her. The resemblance between Elena and her mother was uncanny, from their forest green eyes to the subtle grace in their gestures.

"Are you here for my wife or my daughter, Manuel?" Mr. Foster said from behind me.

I straightened my back and turned to him.

"Stop being petty Jamie and let him in," Mrs. Foster said.

I exhaled in relief as I walked into the room only to come to an abrupt halt when I saw the woman of my dreams. Elena was a vision of beauty in her dress, ending just below her knee. It was as if she had stepped out of a dream, leaving me momentarily breathless.

She crossed her arms and frowned at me. "You're late," she said.

I let out a breath I didn't know I was holding. "And you're gorgeous."

Her eyes twinkled with amusement as she dropped her arms.

"My Mija is beautiful, isn't she?" Mrs. Foster asked as she grabbed her daughter by the shoulders.

Beautiful was an understatement.

Elena's smile lit up the room.

"We'll be helping Cookie if you need us," Mrs. Foster said as she grabbed her husband's hand and left the room. When they left, Elena swiftly locked the door and then leaped into my arms, her lips eagerly finding mine.

The taste of her drove me insane.

"I missed you," she said into the kiss, her breathing quickening. Elena's fingers found their way into my hair, gently pulling me closer, as if we couldn't get any closer.

I pressed her against the wall, our bodies molded together. My heart raced as I felt the softness of her skin against mine, and I couldn't help but marvel at how perfectly we fit together.

Breaking the kiss, I said, "I missed you too."

Elena's eyes sparkled with affection. "I'm a bit nervous. Distract me?"

I stroked her hair. "How am I going to do that?"

She kissed me again and moaned into my lips, pushing me back until I landed on the bed. Then she straddled me to kiss my neck. "I want to suck your cock," she whispered into my ear.

"Woah."

Before I could respond, she sank to her knees and raised my t-shirt. Then she undid my belt. I was hard the moment she kissed me earlier but even that couldn't be compared to how it felt when she pulled down my jeans and stroked me through my underwear.

She pulled it off and my cock sprung free, with precum leaking from the tip. Elena grabbed it with one hand and stroked while the other fished out my balls and massaged them.

I moaned and gripped the sheets, jumping up a little when I felt her tongue wrap itself around the head. "Jesus, that feels so good babe."

My fingers found their way to her hair and I thrusted up so she took more of my cock in her mouth. My breathing sped up, my toes curled and pleasure coursed through my veins as she sucked hard and stroked firmly.

It felt like heaven.

Elena took it with ease and I slid deep down her throat as my fingers sunk deeper into her wavy hair. I looked down at her, at the way her green eyes watched me, the way her tits strained against her dress and my hips moved faster.

"Fuck, yes baby, that's it," I hissed. Drool leaked down from her mouth and I knew I was going to cum soon.

I slipped out of her mouth quickly and pulled her up. Elena gasped and her eyes sparkled with desire. I pulled down the straps of her dress, freeing her tits and teased her nipples with quick bites. She squirmed against me.

I reached beneath her skirt and slid her thong to the side. "When you go out there, I don't want you thinking of anything but me," I said.

She moaned. "Manny."

My fingers stroked her pussy before moving over to her clit. She was so wet, so desperate and it was for me. "I want you thinking of all the different ways I'll fuck you after the show. You want that, don't you?"

She nodded, whimpers escaping her lips in short gasps.

I dragged her hips to the edge of the bed and bent down further. Before burying my face between her legs. Her pussy was hot and went against my lips, feeling me with the instant desire to have more, to taste more.

I turned my head and my tongue flicked sideways across her clit. Elena's moan was so loud, she covered her mouth and her body shivered with pleasure. I reached up and rolled one nipple between my thumb and forefinger while I sucked her clit. Her body tightened and she grinded her lips against my mouth.

"Yes, Manny. Oh God yes," She gasped.

I licked quickly, lapping up her juices, and she balled her fists around my hair. With every shiver and every twitch, it wasn't long until she threw her head back and came all over my face.

I rubbed her clit and pulled away, watching her pant and come down from her high, even as her body screamed for me. I lay my head on her thigh and she looked down at me.

"Was that good enough of a distraction for you?" I asked.

"You're insufferable," she said playfully.

I laughed and stood, helping her adjust her dress.

"Cookie should be here with the makeup artist soon," she said. "You'll sit with my parents, right? I want to be able to see you."

I smiled down at her. "You'll see me," I said.

***

I sat in the elegant hall, my eyes drifting occasionally to the watch on my wrist. The atmosphere was charged with anticipation, the room filled with well-dressed attendees sipping champagne and chatting in hushed tones. The ambiance was rich, with chandeliers casting a warm glow over the attendees, and elegant curtains framing the stage.

A server offered me a glass of champagne, which I took absent-mindedly, my mind preoccupied with thoughts of Elena's upcoming performance. I had grown to love seeing her on stage, watching her be a star.

Suddenly, the curtains on the stage parted, and the room erupted in cheers and applause. My heart raced as I took a sip of the drink. But to my surprise, it wasn't Elena who appeared under the spotlight.

It was Cookie.

Cookie's smile appeared forced as she stood before the expectant crowd. She held a microphone and spoke, her voice carrying through the room. "Ladies and gentlemen, I apologize for the delay. Unfortunately, we're experiencing some technical difficulties, and Elena's performance will be delayed."

A low murmur coursed through the audience. I could feel the tension in the room, and I exchanged a concerned look with Elena's parents, who were sitting beside me.

Jamie Foster leaned in, his voice low. "Manuel, do you know what's happening?"

I shook my head. "I have no idea, but I'll find out."

Cookie exited the stage. I rose from my seat and followed her backstage. As I tapped her shoulder, she flinched, and her eyes met mine with a mix of relief and worry.

"What's going on?" I asked.

Cookie glanced around. Then she sighed before speaking, "Okay, don't panic."

My eyebrows shot up. "Why would I panic?"

She hesitated for a moment, choosing her words carefully. "Elena... she's gone."

My heart felt like it had dropped into my stomach. "Gone? What the hell do you mean, gone?"

Before Cookie could respond, Tony, the guy I had met at the hospital, jogged up to us. He looked equally concerned. "I can't find her," he said, his voice trembling. "I've been looking everywhere."

I felt a shiver of dread crawl up my spine. "You mean you can't find Elena?"

Cookie nodded, her expression heavy with worry. "She went to use the restroom, but when she didn't come back, I got concerned. Now we have security out looking for her."

My phone was already in my hand, and I quickly dialed Elena's number. My heart hammered in my chest as I listened to it ring, praying for her to pick up.

The tension in the air was suffocating as Cookie and Tony discussed Elena's disappearance. Just then, a security guard walked up to us, clearly distressed.

"We've got a complication," he said, his voice strained.

I noticed a man standing next to the security guard. He held a tablet and gestured to Cookie. "Sorry, ma'am," he began, "I didn't recognize the man when he first came in."

Cookie stared at the screen for a moment and then she glared at the man. "You had a blacklist for a reason, to know who not to let in!" She yelled.

The man stammered, "I apologize; it was a mistake."

My eyes were fixed on the footage on the tablet, and I saw who the man in it was.

Caleb.

Anger surged through me. "How the hell did he get in?" I asked, dropping my phone.

The man stammered out an apology, and I had the urge to punch him in the face. But instead, I decided to try calling Elena again. No response.

"I'm going to find her myself," I declared.

If Caleb was in the hotel, she was not safe.

"Wait, Manny," Cookie urged, reaching out to grab my arm, "we don't know if Caleb has something to do with this yet."

Before I could respond, there was a deafening commotion. A loud boom echoed through the hotel, shaking the very foundation. My eyes widened, and I turned to Cookie.

"What's going on?" she asked, her eyes filled with concern.

Amidst the chaos, a frantic woman ran past us, shouting, "Fire!"

The security man listened on his walkie-talkie. Then he turned to us. "There's a gas leak in the hotel and there have been two different explosions. We need to evacuate everyone immediately."

"But what about Elena?" Cookie asked.

She was right. What about Elena?

Without a word, I left her behind and sprinted towards the area where the restrooms were located. The scent of gas and smoke hung heavily in the air as I walked in. It was dangerous to be in the vicinity, but I needed to find Elena.

My heart pounded as I went through all the restroom stalls, desperately searching for her. Panic set in as I found nothing, and I rushed back outside, just in time to be met with another deafening explosion. The entire hotel seemed to shake, and I could see the flicker of flames from the nearby emergency exit.

Realization hit me like a punch to the gut. Someone was setting off these explosions deliberately, and they were getting closer. Just as I was about to run the other way, I heard a piercing scream.

"Elena..." I muttered.

Without a second thought, I flung the door open.

The intense heat of the fire licked at my skin as I stepped inside, the acrid smoke stinging my eyes and throat. "Elena!" I called out repeatedly, my voice hoarse with desperation.

"Elena!"

"Manny!" I heard her faint voice. "Oh God, it's you."

I followed her voice toward her location and found her under the stairwell, tied helplessly to a pole, her terrified eyes locking onto mine.

"He's here, Manny," Elena said as I freed her from the ropes, my fingers trembling with urgency. "Caleb is here. He tied me up and left me to burn."

"Stay close to me," I told her, my voice firm as I helped her to her feet. "We're getting out of here."

We rushed back toward the emergency exit, but as we emerged into the smoky corridor, I spotted a new threat. Smoke was billowing from the direction of the ballroom. I turned to Elena.

"We need to take the stair to get to another floor," I explained, but another violent shake of the building interrupted me. "We have to move, Elena, before this place collapses."

She nodded and we sprinted toward the stairs, taking them two at a time until we reached the lowest floor. When we stepped onto the floor, the sight of a crowd escaping the building made me feel relieved. If we could get out, then we would be fine.

Elena and I made our way towards the entrance, pushing past the sea of bodies. Then suddenly, a gunshot rang out, followed by screams, and people around us fell to the floor.

Elena and I dropped down, huddling behind a nearby pillar. Fear coursed through me but it quickly turned to rage when I saw Caleb walk up to us with a gun. As the panicked crowd fled the building, his eyes locked on Elena and me with a chilling intensity.

"The fireman saves you again," Caleb's voice was dripping with venom as his gaze shifted to me. "You're becoming annoying."

"What are you going to do about it?" I asked, blocking Elena's body with mine. "Shoot me in front of all these people?"

He sneered. "You think I care? You know nothing. You're new in Elena's life. You have no idea who I am to her. She wouldn't be the superstar she is without my help. I made her and she left me!"

"You cheated and robbed me," Elena said angrily.

"You owe me!" Caleb yelled. The security team had encircled him, urging him to put the weapon down, but he pointed it directly at her. "You owe me everything that you are today. You know it but you ruined my career and everything I built over this. I came to this stupid town with you and now I can't even go back to New York because of you!"

Elena didn't flinch, her resolve unbroken. "You're surrounded, Caleb. Drop the gun."

He chuckled bitterly. "No, I already lost. But I'm not losing alone."

He motioned to pull the trigger and Elena screamed while I wrapped my body around hers. A gunshot echoed in the room and it took me a few seconds to look up and realize Caleb wasn't the one who shot. I watched him cry out in pain, clutching his leg as he collapsed to the floor.

As Caleb fell to the ground, writhing in pain from the gunshot wound, my eyes shifted upward to see one of Elena's security team members holding a smoking gun. The rest of the team quickly closed in on Caleb, swiftly disarming him and restraining him.

Elena's body tensed next to me and I turned to hold her. She buried her face in my neck.

"It's okay. You're okay," I mumbled, even though my heart was pounding in my chest.

While the commotion continued around us, one of the security personnel approached us He asked if he could escort us safely out of the premises. Elena clung to my side as we stood, and I nodded in agreement. We followed the security officer out of the chaotic scene, Elena's arm wrapped around mine as we made our way to safety.

We stepped out of the hotel and came face-to-face with her parents and Cookie amidst the crowd. Elena ran toward them and as I watched her, I realized the events of the evening had only reinforced one thing for me – I never wanted to let her go.

CHAPTER TWENTY

ELENA

The night was cool and tranquil as Manny and I walked together, the soft glow of streetlights casting long shadows on the pavement. He was engrossed in his phone for a moment, and I couldn't resist stealing a glance at him. His brows were scrunched together seriously while his lips pressed into a thin line. There was something about his presence that made me feel safe, no matter what was going on around me.

Manny must have sensed my gaze because he suddenly looked up, his eyes lighting up with a warm smile. He eagerly turned his phone toward me, revealing a picture of us at an award show. "It's my favorite," he said.

I couldn't help but chuckle at the memory – I had insisted he come as my date, and he'd reluctantly agreed. As it turned out, he had enjoyed the evening far more than he initially let on.

"Why is this your favorite?" I asked.

Manny's smile only widened, and he shrugged playfully. "Your eyes are on me, not the camera. You're looking at me like you're in love with me."

I couldn't find the words to respond. The truth was, I was in love with him. In the weeks that followed Caleb's arrest, Manny had been my constant support. His playful and lighthearted nature had become a comforting presence in my life. I remembered the moment when he had asked me to be his girlfriend, over a cup of smoothie, no less. I had been so surprised that I had nearly choked on it, and Manny's laughter had filled the room as he patted my back, teasing me about my reaction.

As we continued our nighttime stroll, I realized that being with Manny brought a sense of joy and contentment I hadn't known in a long time. It wasn't just the laughter and the fun, but the way he made me feel cherished and safe. So yes, I was definitely in love with him. But sometimes, words had a way of escaping me, and all I could do was smile back at him, letting my heart do the talking.

We stopped in front of Manny's house, and I turned to him, curiosity tugging at my heart. "Manny," I began, "why do you want me to be in love with you so badly?"

He flashed me a warm smile as he led me towards the front door. "Because I'm in love with you," he confessed with a hint of playfulness. "And I want you to be in love with me."

As I stepped inside his house, I couldn't help but feel a sense of awe. I glanced back at him, my question lingering in the air. "What are you talking about?"

Manny flicked on the lights and closed the door behind us. He turned to me. "Are you spending the night?" he asked, catching me off guard.

I blinked, my mind racing. Ignoring him, I said, "You told me you've never been in a relationship. How could you know what love is?"

There was a hint of doubt in my voice.

He sighed, his smile unwavering. "I didn't," he admitted. "But now I think I do."

He took a step closer, his gaze locked onto mine. "I think about you all the time. I constantly want to see you. When you're not around, it feels like there's a big part of me that's missing. So, if that's not love, then I don't know what it is."

His words hung in the air, and I was left speechless. The sincerity in his eyes, the way he made my heart flutter – it was all undeniable. As he drew nearer, I inhaled sharply and his scent overwhelmed me.

"Oh," I uttered in surprise as he held my hand, my heart racing.

He quirked an eyebrow and asked, "Is 'oh' all you have to say?"

I felt my face heat up and I could tell a blush had colored my cheeks. I hesitated before murmuring under my breath, "I love you too."

Manny leaned in closer, a playful grin on his lips. "What was that, Star?" He asked. "I didn't hear you," he teased.

I swallowed the lump in my throat and summoned the courage to say it louder, "I love you too."

With a chuckle, he leaned in, pressing his soft, warm lips pressed against mine, and I could taste the faint hint of his favorite lip balm. The kiss began gently, a sweet exploration but then our tongues met in a slow, sensual dance, a rhythmic exchange of desire and passion. I could feel the heat rising within me, a burning need that only he could quench. His hands found their way to my waist, pulling me closer, our bodies pressed tightly together.

When he finally released me, Manny grinned and said, "You should say it again."

I smiled back at him, my heart overflowing with emotion. "I love you," I repeated.

His eyes sparkled with joy, and he whispered, "Now that I've heard it, I don't think I'll ever get over it."

He leaned in for another kiss, sealing our love with every tender touch of our lips.

EPILOGUE
ONE YEAR LATER
ELENA

Sitting in the crowd at the award show, I took deep breaths, trying to calm my racing heart. The moment I had been both excited and anxious about had finally arrived. The announcers were about to reveal the winner for the Album of the Year category, the last album of the night, and I couldn't help but wish that Manny was here with me. After all, he had been the inspiration for so many of the songs on that album.

But Manny was back in Baileys Harbor and I was in New York. I missed him so much that our facetime calls weren't enough anymore and a part of me wanted to be done with the show so I could go back home.

Home. Baileys Harbor was now my home.

Beside me, Cookie glanced up from her tablet, giving me an encouraging smile. "Stop being nervous Elena," she whispered.

I sighed as the announcers called out the nominees for the category. "But what if I don't win?"

She chuckled softly. "Then the judges have no taste in music."

Her words made me laugh, easing some of my tension. But it quickly came back when one of the announcers cleared her throat and said, "And the winner is..."

My heart felt like it was about to leap out of my chest.

"Elena Foster!"

The entire crowd erupted in cheers and applause and my eyes widened. The said my name. Cookie excitedly squealed, tapping my shoulder and pushing me off my chair.

I stood.

Taking cautious steps in my heels, I made my way towards the stage. One of the announcers offered a hand to help me climb the steps, and one of my songs began to play loudly through the speakers. I took the award with trembling hands, facing the microphone with a smile.

The bright lights of the award show stage illuminated my face as I took a moment to gather my thoughts. "First of all," I began, my voice steady but filled with sincerity, "I want to thank everyone who was involved in the production of this album, from the incredibly talented producers to the dedicated members who worked tirelessly behind the scenes. Tony, Frank, and my amazing manager Cookie, I couldn't have done this without you."

The crowd erupted in applause, and I smiled as I continued, "I also want to express my deepest gratitude to my family, who has been my unwavering support system throughout my career. You've believed in me even when I had doubts, and I'm endlessly thankful for your love."

I paused, my gaze turning toward the screen in the back of the stage. "And to my biggest inspiration, the one who isn't here tonight but is always in my heart," I said, my voice softening with emotion. "Manny, you've been my muse and my rock. Every song, every note, every lyric—they all have a piece of you. This award is not just mine; it's ours."

The crowd cheered again. Tears welled up in my eyes as I continued, "And to my incredible fans, you mean the world to me. Your support and love have carried me through the highs and lows of this journey. I promise to keep making music that speaks to your hearts. Thank you."

As I motioned to walk off the stage, I heard a voice say, "Is this thing on?"

My heart raced, and I froze in place, my eyes darting around in disbelief. The words came from the big screen, and I turned to see Manny's face there.

My eyes widened, and tears welled up as I saw him.

The announcers on stage didn't seem taken aback at all. In fact, they wore knowing smiles, as if they had planned this moment. I was left breathless, my attention solely fixed on the screen.

Manny took a deep breath. "If you're seeing this, that means you've won, Elena," he said. "But honestly, I'm not surprised because you're a star. Stars always shine, just like you do. Sometimes, I can't look away from you because of how brightly you're smiling."

I blinked away tears. I missed him so much.

He continued, "I want you to know that this past year with you has been the best year of my life. Before you, life was exciting, but with you, it's worth so much more. Lately, I've been thinking about how I want to do this forever. So, I have just one question..."

The crowd erupted into cheers, their enthusiasm echoing through the room. I turned to see Manny, dressed impeccably, walking up toward me. My eyes widened as he came to a halt in front of me and gracefully dropped to one knee.

I gripped the award in my hand. "What are you doing?"

He grinned playfully. "Asking you to marry me."

He pulled out a small box from his pocket. My heart was racing, and I could hardly believe what was happening. He opened the box, revealing a dazzling ring that sparkled in the spotlight.

My breath caught in my throat as he asked, "So, will you marry me?"

I felt like I might burst from happiness, and my eyes welled up with tears. I nodded vigorously, unable to find my voice. The crowd erupted into cheers, the sound echoing through the venue.

Manny gently slipped the ring onto my finger, and it fit perfectly, as if it had always belonged there. He stood up, and without hesitation, his lips met mine in a sweet and passionate kiss.

In that moment, surrounded by adoring fans and the man I loved, I realized that I had never felt happier in all my years of stardom.

ALSO, BY

T.S. FOX

If you have not read my first book: "Bad Boy Fireman Next Door" here
a link:

    https://www.amazon.com/dp/B0CCLRBSGZ

    Book 2: "Bad Boy Fireman Daddy"

    https://www.amazon.com/dp/B0CDSS8CB8

    Book 3: "Bad Boy Fireman Rescue"

    https://www.amazon.com/dp/B0CH53LMKW

Made in the USA
Middletown, DE
06 January 2024

47365311R00088